The Librarian's Legacy

Preserving the Past to Protect the Future

Rowan Hartley

Table of Contents

Chapter 1
The Library's Silence

The Blythewood Public Library stood at the heart of the town square, a shadow of its former self. Its grand facade, once a beacon of knowledge and community, was now dulled by time. The intricate carvings framing its heavy oak doors were chipped, and the stained-glass windows no longer sparkled as they once had. Ella Carter hesitated at the entrance, her fingers brushing against the smooth brass handle. She always felt a mix of comfort and sadness stepping into this place—a place that had been her refuge and her playground growing up, now reduced to an echo of the lively sanctuary it used to be.

The heavy door creaked as she pushed it open, the sound reverberating through the cavernous room. The library smelled the same: a familiar blend of aged paper, polished wood, and a faint trace of lavender, though no one could ever explain its source. Ella paused in the doorway, her gaze sweeping over the empty tables and dim corners. Once, the library had been filled with life. Children had sprawled on colorful rugs in the reading corner, their laughter mingling with the gentle hum of Mrs. Pearlson's voice as she read aloud. Students had crowded around the long tables, their heads bent together over textbooks and notes. Now, it was quiet. Too quiet.

Ella walked slowly down the main aisle, her sneakers squeaking faintly on the polished floorboards. The silence pressed against her, amplifying her thoughts. She stopped in front of the biography section, her favorite spot as a child. The shelves here loomed taller than the others, their dark wood towering over her like ancient sentinels. She ran her fingers along the spines of the books, their worn edges a testament to years of use.

"Ella," a voice called softly from the front desk, pulling her from her thoughts.

Mrs. Pearlson sat in her usual spot, surrounded by untidy stacks of papers and faded books. Her silver hair was neatly pinned back, but her face bore the weight of exhaustion. She looked up over the rim of her glasses, offering a tired smile.

"You're here early again," she said, her voice warm despite her weary expression.

Ella shrugged, shoving her hands into the pockets of her hoodie. "It's peaceful when it's quiet."

"Peaceful, yes." Mrs. Pearlson's eyes drifted toward the empty children's corner, a flicker of sadness crossing her face. "But quiet can be a curse, too."

Ella tilted her head, curiosity stirring. "What do you mean?"

Mrs. Pearlson leaned back in her chair, sighing deeply. "This place used to be alive, Ella. People would come here not just for books, but for each other. It was a hub for the town—a place where everyone belonged. Now... now it feels like a relic. Forgotten."

Ella frowned, shifting her weight. "But it still matters, doesn't it? To some people?"

"To some," Mrs. Pearlson agreed, though her tone was heavy. She began shuffling through the papers on her desk, her movements slow and deliberate. "But the council doesn't see it that way. They think libraries are unnecessary in this day and age. A waste of resources."

Ella's chest tightened. She had heard whispers about the library's closure, but hearing Mrs. Pearlson confirm it made it feel all the more real. "They're really going to close it?" she asked, her voice barely above a whisper.

Mrs. Pearlson nodded grimly. "That's what they've decided. Unless, by some miracle, we can prove its worth to the town. But miracles are hard to come by these days."

Ella's gaze dropped to the worn floorboards, her mind racing. She couldn't imagine the library being gone. It was more than a building to her; it was a part of her history, her identity. Her grandmother had brought her here every week as a child, teaching her to love stories and the worlds they created.

"I won't let them," she said suddenly, the words slipping out before she could stop them.

Mrs. Pearlson looked at her, a soft smile tugging at the corners of her mouth. "You've always had a fighting spirit, Ella. But some battles are bigger than us."

Ella said nothing, the weight of the librarian's words settling heavily on her. She turned back toward the biography section, her fingers trailing along the spines of the books once more. As she reached the far end of the shelf, something caught her eye. A thin crack ran along the edge of the wood paneling, just barely visible in the dim light. She crouched down, inspecting it more closely. The panel seemed loose, as if it had shifted out of place over time.

Her heart quickened. What was behind it? A forgotten book? A hidden compartment? She hesitated, glancing over her shoulder toward Mrs. Pearlson, who was now absorbed in her paperwork. Part of her wanted to investigate right then and there, but another part whispered caution. Instead, she filed the detail away in her mind, a small seed of curiosity taking root.

Ella straightened and stepped back, her gaze lingering on the panel for a moment longer before turning away. As she walked toward the front desk, she resolved to come back later. Whatever was hidden there, it felt important—like a secret waiting to be uncovered.

The library hummed with a quiet stillness as she left, the weight of its history and its uncertain future pressing against her. For the first time, Ella felt the stirrings of something she hadn't felt in a long time: a sense of purpose.

The library was quiet, save for the soft scratching of Mrs. Pearlson's pen against paper as she worked through her endless stack of overdue notices. Ella sat across from her at the desk, her chin propped up on her hand as she idly traced patterns in the wood grain. The conversation about the library's closure lingered in the air like a heavy fog, and Ella couldn't shake the tightness in her chest.

"You really think there's no way to save it?" Ella asked, breaking the silence.

Mrs. Pearlson paused, her pen hovering mid-air. She adjusted her glasses and looked at Ella, her expression softening. "I didn't say that. But saving it would take more than a good intention, my dear. It would take… something extraordinary."

Ella frowned. "Like what? A petition? A fundraiser? There has to be something."

Mrs. Pearlson gave a weary chuckle. "Oh, petitions and fundraisers—they're all well and good, but they don't always speak to the heart. This library needs more than money or signatures. It needs people to remember why it matters in the first place."

"That's what I mean!" Ella leaned forward, her eyes bright. "If we remind people why it's important, why they love it, maybe they'll fight for it. Maybe the council will listen."

Mrs. Pearlson tilted her head, studying her for a moment. "You remind me so much of Evelyn Blythe," she said softly.

Ella blinked, caught off guard. "Mrs. Blythe? The first librarian?"

"That's right." Mrs. Pearlson set her pen down and leaned back in her chair, her gaze distant as if looking into the past. "Evelyn wasn't just a librarian. She was a dreamer, a believer in the power of stories and what they could do for people. She always said this library wasn't just a building—it was alive. A place with a soul."

Ella tilted her head, intrigued. "What did she mean by that? 'A place with a soul'?"

Mrs. Pearlson smiled wistfully. "She used to say the library held secrets. That if you listened closely enough, it would speak to you. Of course, people laughed—called her fanciful, eccentric. But Evelyn didn't care. She believed every book here carried a piece of its reader with it, and together, they made the library more than just walls and shelves."

"That's…" Ella hesitated, searching for the right word. "Beautiful."

"It was." Mrs. Pearlson's voice was thick with emotion. "Evelyn poured her heart into this place. She built it for everyone, not just for reading but for connection. For discovery. She used to tell me, 'Pearlson, one day, someone will find what this library has been waiting to show them.'"

Ella sat back, her mind buzzing. "What does that mean? 'Find what the library has been waiting to show them?'"

"I don't know," Mrs. Pearlson admitted, shaking her head. "Evelyn was full of mysteries. She passed before she could explain, but I've always wondered if she left something behind—a part of herself in this place."

Ella stared at the desk, her thoughts racing. She remembered the loose panel she'd noticed earlier, the way it seemed out of place. Could it be connected to what Mrs. Blythe had believed? The idea sent a thrill of excitement through her.

"My grandmother used to tell me about Mrs. Blythe," Ella said suddenly. "She said she was the reason she fell in love with books. That when she was a little girl, Mrs. Blythe would sit her down in the reading corner and tell her stories—stories she made up on the spot."

Mrs. Pearlson chuckled. "That sounds like Evelyn. She had a gift for storytelling, even without a book in her hand. She could make you believe in magic, in possibilities."

Ella smiled, the tightness in her chest easing slightly. "My grandmother always said Mrs. Blythe believed in me, even before I was born. She used to tell me, 'Ella, if Evelyn Blythe were here, she'd say you've got a spark—a bit of the magic she always talked about.'"

"She was right." Mrs. Pearlson's eyes twinkled as she leaned forward, resting her elbows on the desk. "You do have a spark, Ella. You're curious, determined. Just like Evelyn. Maybe that's why this place still calls to you."

Ella's smile faltered, replaced by a thoughtful expression. "Do you think that's true? That the library… calls to people?"

Mrs. Pearlson nodded slowly. "I do. And I think it's calling to you now. Maybe you're meant to find what Evelyn left behind."

Ella swallowed hard, her heart pounding. "But what if I can't? What if I'm not the one?"

Mrs. Pearlson reached out and covered Ella's hand with her own, her touch warm and reassuring. "The fact that you care, Ella—that you're asking these questions—tells me you're exactly the one."

For a moment, they sat in silence, the weight of the conversation settling between them. Ella glanced back toward the biography section, her thoughts returning to the loose panel. If Mrs. Blythe had truly left something behind, maybe—just maybe—it was waiting for her to find.

"I won't let them take this place," Ella said finally, her voice steady. "Whatever it takes, I'll find a way to save it."

Mrs. Pearlson smiled, a glimmer of hope lighting her tired eyes. "If anyone can, it's you, my dear. Evelyn would be proud."

The late afternoon sun filtered weakly through the stained-glass windows of Blythewood Library, casting fragmented patterns of light on the worn floorboards. Ella sat cross-legged in her favorite corner, nestled beneath the towering shelves of the biography section. This had always been her spot—the place she came to think, to breathe, to feel the library's quiet magic. Today, though, the silence felt heavier, pressing down on her with the weight of Mrs. Pearlson's words.

Ella ran her fingers over the spines of the books nearest her, the familiar texture of cracked leather and embossed gold lettering grounding her. She remembered sitting here as a little girl, listening to her grandmother's soft voice as she read from these very shelves. Back then, the library had seemed endless, like a world all its own. Now, it felt like a relic, a fragile thread connecting her to something slipping away.

Her gaze wandered to the corner of the shelf where she'd noticed the crack in the wood earlier. She shifted onto her knees, leaning closer to examine it. The faint line ran along the panel's edge, almost invisible unless you were looking for it. Ella hesitated, her heart quickening. Was this just a quirk of the old wood, or was it something more?

She reached out, her fingertips brushing against the seam. The panel wobbled slightly under her touch, and a soft creak broke the stillness. Ella glanced over her shoulder, half-expecting Mrs. Pearlson to appear and scold her. But the library remained silent, its shadows pooling in the corners.

Her curiosity burned brighter. With a quick glance to make sure she was alone, she pressed her palms firmly against the panel and pushed. It gave way with a faint click, revealing a narrow gap behind it. Ella froze, her breath caught in her throat. She hadn't expected it to actually move.

For a moment, she hesitated. What if this was nothing—just an empty space left by the shifting wood? But what if it wasn't? The idea of discovering something hidden, something meant to be found, sent a thrill through her. Slowly, carefully, she slid the panel aside.

Behind it was a small hollow, lined with dust and cobwebs. Nestled within was a thin, leather-bound book. The cover was faded, its edges worn smooth by time, but intricate gold designs still traced its surface. Ella reached in and pulled it free, her hands trembling slightly. She turned it over, brushing away the layer of dust that clung to the cover.

The book was heavier than it looked, its leather cool under her fingers. She opened it gingerly, the spine creaking in protest. Inside, the first page was blank, but the second held something that made her breath hitch. In looping, elegant handwriting, a single phrase was scrawled across the top of the page:

"To those who seek the library's soul, follow the map, and you will find what has been hidden."

Ella stared at the words, her mind racing. "The library's soul?" she whispered aloud. The phrase echoed Mrs. Pearlson's earlier story about Evelyn Blythe and her belief in the library's magic. Could this be connected?

She turned the page, her pulse quickening. On the next sheet was a hand-drawn map, its lines delicate and precise. It depicted the library in intricate detail, every shelf and corner painstakingly sketched. Symbols dotted the blueprint—stars, swirls, and crosses scattered across the map like breadcrumbs. Some were in places Ella recognized, like the biography section and the reading room, while others marked areas she'd never paid attention to.

"What is this?" she murmured, tracing the lines with her fingertip. The ink was faded but still legible, the symbols seeming to pulse with a quiet energy. Ella's thoughts tumbled over one another. Had Evelyn Blythe drawn this? Was this the secret Mrs. Pearlson had spoken of—the thing the library was waiting to show someone?

The idea filled her with a mix of wonder and trepidation. If this map was real, if it truly led to something hidden within the library, then why had it been left undiscovered for so long? Why her?

She closed the book gently, hugging it to her chest. The weight of it felt significant, as though it held more than just paper and ink. Ella sat back against the shelf, her mind racing with possibilities. The library had always been her sanctuary, but now it felt like something more. A mystery, a puzzle, waiting to be solved.

Her grandmother's voice echoed in her memory: "Evelyn Blythe believed this library had a soul. Maybe one day, you'll find it too." Ella's grip on the book tightened. Maybe this was what her grandmother had meant. Maybe this was why she had always felt so drawn to this place.

Ella stood slowly, glancing toward the front desk where Mrs. Pearlson was still absorbed in her paperwork. She didn't want to share the discovery just yet—not until she understood what it meant. Instead, she slipped the book into her bag, her mind already leaping ahead to what the map might reveal.

As she walked toward the exit, the library seemed to hum softly around her, the faint scent of lavender drifting through the air. For the first time in months, Ella felt a spark of hope. The library wasn't just a relic of the past. It was alive, and it was speaking to her.

Chapter 2
Echoes of Evelyn Blythe

The town hall was filled to bursting, the air thick with murmurs and tension. Blythewood's residents had come in force, squeezing into rows of creaky wooden chairs, their expressions ranging from frustration to quiet unease. A low buzz of conversation bounced off the high ceilings, a murmur of anxious questions and half-formed arguments.

Ella sat near the back, wedged between Max and Jada. Her fingers twisted nervously in her lap as she scanned the room. She recognized nearly everyone—Mr. Patel from the antique shop, the Bennett twins who ran the bakery, parents, teachers, and older residents who had lived in Blythewood their entire lives. Noah lingered a few rows ahead, his arms crossed tightly over his chest as he stared at the empty podium.

"This is bad," Jada whispered beside her, her voice low and urgent. "You can feel it already."

Ella nodded faintly, her stomach knotting. Across the room, Mrs. Pearlson sat near the aisle, her hands folded tightly in her lap, her face pale but resolute. She looked so small, so fragile, among the crowd.

"Relax," Max muttered, though his restless knee bounced beneath the chair. "Maybe he'll just say the library needs a fresh coat of paint."

But even Max's attempt at humor fell flat. The room went silent as Mayor Grayson appeared, flanked by two council members. He walked with a kind of purposeful calm that made Ella's throat tighten. He adjusted his glasses, surveyed the crowd, and took his place behind the podium.

"Good evening, everyone," the mayor began, his voice measured and practiced, as though he were delivering a weather report rather than a life-changing decision. "Thank you for coming tonight. I know many of you have concerns about the state of our town—about the future of Blythewood and what must be done to ensure its survival."

A few heads nodded cautiously. Ella watched as the mayor's gaze swept the room, his expression unreadable.

"Over the past several months, the council has worked tirelessly to find solutions to our economic struggles," Grayson continued, his tone growing heavier. "It's no secret that Blythewood has faced hard times. Our businesses have dwindled, our town has fallen behind, and there are difficult choices we can no longer avoid."

A murmur rippled through the crowd. Ella felt a pit open in her stomach. She already knew where this was going, but hearing it said aloud was worse than she imagined.

"To that end," Mayor Grayson said, his voice cutting through the rising noise, "the council has voted to approve the sale of the Blythewood Public Library and its surrounding land to private developers."

The room exploded into chaos.

"What?" someone shouted from the back.

"You can't be serious!" cried another voice, shrill with disbelief.

"No!" Mrs. Pearlson's voice cut through the din like a blade. She was on her feet, her face flushed with anger. "You can't just sell it. That library has been part of this town for generations!"

The mayor held up his hands, trying to regain control. "Please, everyone—please. Let me explain."

"Explain?" Mr. Patel's voice rose over the crowd. "How do you explain selling our history? That library *is* Blythewood!"

"You're selling our heart!" a woman near the front added, her voice trembling.

The mayor's face tightened, his calm facade beginning to crack. "I understand your emotions," he said firmly, though his voice lacked warmth. "But emotions don't keep our town running. The developers have promised to build something new, something that will bring jobs, tourists, and resources back to Blythewood."

"And where will the children go?" Mrs. Pearlson shot back. "Where will the community gather? Do you think a strip mall can replace a place like this?"

"Pearlson—"

"No!" Her voice wavered, but her resolve did not. "This isn't just a building, Elliot. You know that. You *know* what that library means to people."

The mayor's jaw clenched, his glasses catching the light as he looked away. "Times change," he said quietly. "We have to change with them."

The murmurs shifted, breaking into quiet arguments among the townspeople. Some older residents were shaking their heads, their faces pinched with betrayal. Others sat silently, their eyes fixed on their laps.

"This isn't fair," Ella whispered, her voice shaking.

"It's wrong," Max growled, his fists clenching at his sides. "They can't just—can't just sell it like it doesn't matter."

Jada glanced nervously at the crowd. "Not everyone's upset," she murmured. Ella followed her gaze and saw a handful of people nodding reluctantly—parents, younger shop owners, even a few of their teachers.

"They're desperate," Jada continued. "They think a new development will fix everything."

"It won't," Ella said sharply. "It'll ruin what's left."

Up at the podium, Mayor Grayson continued. "The decision is final. The sale will proceed at the end of the month unless another solution can be presented—one that addresses the town's financial needs."

The words hit Ella like a punch. *Unless another solution can be presented.*

"So that's it, then?" Mrs. Pearlson demanded, her voice brittle. "You're giving us a deadline to save what's left of this town's heart?"

The mayor didn't respond. Instead, he gave a curt nod and stepped back, leaving the townspeople to argue among themselves.

Ella felt like the room was closing in around her. Max turned to her, his expression intense. "Ella, we can't let this happen."

She gripped the edge of her seat, her nails biting into the wood. "We won't," she said, her voice barely more than a whisper. She looked across the room at Mrs. Pearlson, who had slumped back into her seat, her face pale and her eyes distant.

"We have to find a way," Ella said. "If we don't…"

She trailed off, the words too heavy to finish.

Max leaned forward, his voice low but urgent. "What about the book? The map? If Mrs. Blythe hid something—maybe something important—this could be our chance."

Ella's pulse quickened, the idea sparking like flint against stone. *The map. The library's soul.*

"I think you're right," she said, meeting Max's gaze. "If there's even the smallest chance we can save the library, we have to take it."

Jada exhaled, pulling her sketchbook into her lap. "Well," she said softly, "it sounds like we have work to do."

The three of them sat in silence as the voices of the crowd swirled around them, a storm of anger, fear, and resignation. But amidst it all, Ella felt something solid take root inside her—a determination that steadied her hands and cleared her thoughts.

The library wasn't gone yet. And she wasn't going to let it go without a fight.

The sun had begun its descent, casting Blythewood in hues of orange and purple, but the chill in the air didn't match the sky's warmth. Ella sat on the library steps, her back against the cold stone wall, knees drawn up as her pencil scratched across the page of her notebook. She'd torn a blank sheet from the back, its edges rough and uneven, but that didn't matter. The map she'd found in the ledger was now taking shape in careful lines beneath her hand.

Her breath fogged in front of her face as she worked, her eyes flicking between the faded marks in the book and the recreation she was sketching. Each line felt like a promise, each symbol a small beacon of hope she clung to. Stars, circles, and cryptic swirls marked places in the library—places she didn't yet understand but knew mattered. The words from the first page of the ledger whispered back to her: *"Follow the map to find the library's soul."*

"Are you planning on opening a cartography business or something?"

Ella flinched as Max dropped onto the step beside her, his backpack thudding against the stone. He leaned back, arms stretched across the step behind him, his voice carrying its usual teasing tone.

"It's not funny, Max," she said, glancing up for only a moment before turning back to her sketch. "I'm trying to focus."

He tilted his head, peering at the notebook in her lap. "Is that the map you found? Looks like a bunch of squiggles to me."

"They're *not* squiggles," Ella shot back, brushing her hair out of her face. "They're symbols. Clues. And if we figure them out, maybe we can find something important—something that will save the library."

Max was quiet for a beat, watching her hands move with precision. "You really think there's something hidden here? Something worth all of this?"

"I have to believe there is," she said softly, her pencil slowing as she carefully shaded the lines marking the reading room. "If Mrs. Blythe went through the trouble of making this map and writing about the library's soul, then she wanted someone to find it."

Max let out a slow breath, his gaze drifting toward the library's towering doors. "You know, I was kidding earlier, but you're serious about this, huh?"

Ella stopped sketching and looked up at him. "Of course I'm serious. This isn't just about books or dusty shelves. This is *our* library, Max. The place where my grandmother read to me. The place where your mom used to help with storytime when we were little. It's…" She faltered, searching for the right words, her voice quieter now. "It's part of us. It's part of Blythewood."

Max scratched the back of his neck, a flicker of something softening his usual bravado. "Yeah, I guess it is. My mom always says she learned to love reading because of this place." He glanced over at her notebook again. "So what's the plan, then? You're going to find a buried treasure in the broom closet?"

Ella smiled faintly, the smallest hint of relief breaking through her worry. "Maybe not treasure. But if we find something that shows how important this library is—something the mayor and the council can't ignore—then maybe we can stop them."

"And the map is step one."

"Yes." Ella looked down at her sketch, her resolve tightening in her chest. The map felt like a key. What it unlocked, she didn't know yet, but it was more than just a puzzle. It was a chance. A chance to save the only place in town that still felt alive to her.

The library's clock tower loomed high above them, its hands frozen as they had been for years, locked in a time no one seemed to remember. Ella stared up at it, her voice quiet but firm. "We have three weeks until they sell the land."

Max let out a low whistle. "Three weeks isn't much time, El."

"Then we'll have to move fast."

Max studied her for a moment, a grin tugging at his lips. "You're pretty intense when you want to be, you know that?"

Ella looked at him, a smile slipping onto her face despite herself. "Someone has to be."

"Fair point." Max leaned forward, resting his elbows on his knees. "Well, whatever crazy scavenger hunt you're about to drag me into, I'm in."

"You mean it?"

"Yeah, I mean it. Someone's got to keep you out of trouble, right?"

Before Ella could respond, another voice cut in. "What's all the whispering about?"

Jada stood at the base of the steps, her bag slung over one shoulder and her brow quirked in curiosity. "You two look like you're plotting something."

"We are," Max replied with a grin. "Ella found a map. A magical map that's going to save the library."

Jada gave him a skeptical look before turning her attention to Ella. "A map?"

"It's real," Ella said quickly, holding up the ledger and her sketchbook as proof. "Mrs. Blythe left it behind, and it's full of clues. I think she was trying to show us something about the library—something important."

Jada climbed the steps, eyeing the map carefully before sitting down beside them. "This is… interesting. You think the map leads to something hidden in the library?"

"I do," Ella said firmly. "And I think if we find it, we can show the town why this place matters."

Jada looked at her for a long moment, then nodded, a spark of curiosity lighting her eyes. "Okay. I'm in. If there's something worth finding in the library, I'll help you figure it out."

Max clapped his hands together, his grin widening. "And just like that, Team Library is born."

Ella looked between them, her friends, her allies, and felt a flicker of hope burn brighter. She traced one of the symbols on the map again, her determination blooming like a seed finally catching light.

Three weeks. It wasn't much time, but it was enough. It had to be.

<hr>

The library's reading nook felt smaller with all four of them crammed into it. The space was tucked behind the children's wing, a place long forgotten by most visitors but loved by Ella and her friends for its quiet and privacy. The old, threadbare cushions sagged under their weight as they sat in a tight circle, the ledger open on the floor between them like an ancient artifact.

"Okay," Ella said, her voice steady but urgent. "I need you guys to hear me out. All of it."

Max, sprawled out like he owned the place, leaned back against the wall with his hands behind his head. "We're listening, Captain Carter. Lay it on us."

Jada perched cross-legged across from him, sketchbook balanced on her lap, pencil twirling between her fingers. "Go on, Ella. What's the plan?"

Noah sat with his back against the wall, arms crossed over his chest. He hadn't said much since they'd gathered, his brow furrowed as he listened.

Ella took a deep breath and pointed to the open ledger. "This book belonged to Mrs. Blythe—the first librarian. I found it hidden between the shelves yesterday. It's a map of the library, but it's more than that. There are symbols, clues… and a message."

"What kind of message?" Jada asked, leaning forward slightly.

Ella's finger traced the looping words written at the top of the map. "It says, *Follow the map to find the library's soul.*' I think Mrs. Blythe left something behind. Something important."

Max's grin was instant. "A treasure hunt. This is a literal treasure hunt."

"It's not about treasure, Max," Ella shot back. "It's about saving the library. If we find whatever Mrs. Blythe hid—something that proves how important this place is—maybe we can stop the council from selling it."

Jada's pencil stopped mid-spin. "You're serious about this?"

"I'm completely serious." Ella's voice didn't waver. "The library's been here for generations. It's a part of this town, and it's being ripped away because no one cares enough to fight for it. But we can. I know we can."

Max let out an exaggerated breath, eyes sparkling. "I have to say, I didn't expect my week to involve uncovering ancient mysteries, but I'm here for it."

"Of course you're excited," Jada said dryly. "You'd dive headfirst into an empty well if someone told you there might be a secret down there."

"Uh, correction, *if* there was a chance of a secret *treasure* down there," Max replied, grinning as he nudged Jada's arm. "But seriously, this sounds awesome. I mean, come on—a hidden map, clues, maybe even secret passages? Who wouldn't want in?"

Jada shook her head, though a small smile tugged at her lips. "It *does* sound intriguing. I could help with the map—digitize it, overlay it with the current library floor plan. Maybe we can figure out where those symbols lead."

Ella beamed. "That's exactly what I was hoping you'd say."

They both turned to Noah, who hadn't said a word. He sat with his head bowed slightly, eyes fixed on the ledger like it might come alive at any second. Finally, he spoke, his voice low and careful.

"And what if we don't find anything?"

The question hung in the air like a weight. Max's grin faltered, and Jada's pencil stilled. Ella met Noah's gaze and said quietly, "Then at least we tried."

Noah sighed and rubbed the back of his neck. "It's not that I don't want to help. I just..." He trailed off, his shoulders slumping slightly. "I don't see how kids like us are supposed to change anything."

"We can," Ella said firmly. "We *have* to. If we don't fight for the library, who will? Mrs. Pearlson can't do it alone, and the mayor's already made up his mind. It's up to us to prove this place matters."

Max elbowed Noah gently. "Come on, man. You fixed the old treehouse when it was falling apart. If anyone can help us figure out what's hidden in this building, it's you."

"And we need you," Ella added softly. "All of us together. That's the only way this will work."

Noah's gaze lifted, his brown eyes thoughtful as they flicked between his friends. After a long pause, he exhaled sharply and uncrossed his arms. "Fine. I'm in. But if we get caught digging through walls or floors, I'm blaming Max."

"That's fair," Max said quickly. "I'm very blameable."

Jada rolled her eyes. "This is going to be chaos, isn't it?"

"Fun chaos," Max corrected with a grin.

Ella sat back, her shoulders loosening for the first time all day. "Then it's settled. We're going to follow this map, figure out what Mrs. Blythe left behind, and save the library."

Max pumped a fist in the air. "Team Library is go!"

"Please don't call us that," Jada muttered, though she didn't sound as annoyed as she tried to look.

Noah cracked the smallest of smiles. "What's next, Captain Carter?"

Ella glanced down at the map she'd sketched earlier, the symbols standing out like tiny sparks of light. "Tomorrow, we start with the first mark on the map. It's in the biography section. Whatever we find there… it'll be the beginning."

Silence settled over the group, but this time it wasn't heavy. It was expectant. Max drummed his fingers against the cushion, Jada flipped to a clean page in her sketchbook, and Noah studied the map like he was already solving its mysteries in his head.

Ella closed the ledger, holding it carefully in her lap. They were just four kids sitting in a forgotten corner of the library, but for the first time since the announcement, hope didn't feel impossible. It felt like a spark catching fire.

Together, they would save the library. They had to.

Chapter 3
A Map and a Mission

The town hall buzzed with a low hum of murmured voices, the kind that filled the air when people gathered to witness something they didn't fully understand. Ella sat near the back, wedged between Mrs. Pearlson and Max, her foot tapping nervously against the worn wooden floor. The room smelled faintly of dust and varnish, a scent that felt as old as the building itself.

Mayor Grayson stood at the front of the room, his tall frame poised behind the polished podium. His suit was sharp, his glasses catching the glare of the overhead lights as he surveyed the crowd with a practiced calm. Ella recognized that expression. It wasn't the face of someone about to deliver good news.

"Good evening, everyone," Mayor Grayson began, his voice steady and even. He clasped his hands in front of him, exuding a confidence that only made Ella's stomach churn. "Thank you for coming tonight. I know many of you have concerns about the future of Blythewood, and I appreciate the opportunity to address them."

Ella leaned toward Mrs. Pearlson, whispering, "Why does he sound like he's trying to sell something?"

"Because he is," Mrs. Pearlson muttered, her lips pressed into a thin line. "Listen closely."

The mayor adjusted his glasses, glancing at the papers in front of him. "As you all know, Blythewood has faced significant economic challenges in recent years. Businesses have closed, families have moved away, and the town's budget is stretched thinner than ever. We've explored every option to stabilize our finances, and tonight I must share the council's decision regarding one of our most debated assets: the Blythewood Public Library."

Ella stiffened, her heart pounding in her chest. She gripped the edge of her chair, her eyes locked on the mayor.

"To put it plainly," Grayson continued, "the library is no longer financially viable. Its upkeep costs outweigh its usage, and we cannot afford to maintain it any longer. After much deliberation, the council has decided to approve the sale of the library property to private developers."

A ripple of murmurs swept through the room, but it wasn't the uproar Ella had hoped for. Most people simply exchanged glances or shifted uncomfortably in their seats. A few heads nodded in reluctant agreement, while others stared blankly at the mayor as if waiting for him to finish.

Ella shot a glance at Mrs. Pearlson, whose knuckles were white as she gripped her purse. "They can't do this," Ella whispered fiercely. "They can't just sell it."

"It seems they think they can," Mrs. Pearlson replied, her voice tight with restrained anger. "Keep listening."

The mayor raised his hands, signaling for quiet. "I understand that this decision may be difficult for some of you, but it is necessary for the future of Blythewood. The developers have assured us that their project will bring jobs, economic growth, and new opportunities to our town. This isn't just about what we're losing—it's about what we stand to gain."

"What about what we're losing?" Mrs. Pearlson's voice rang out, cutting through the mayor's polished speech like a sharp blade. Heads turned toward her, and Ella felt a surge of pride at the librarian's boldness.

Mayor Grayson's expression flickered for a moment before he recovered, offering her a polite but detached smile. "Mrs. Pearlson, I assure you, the council did not make this decision lightly. We recognize the library's history and its value to the community, but sentimentality alone cannot justify its continued operation."

"Sentimentality?" Mrs. Pearlson repeated, her voice rising. "This library is more than a building. It's a cornerstone of this town—a place where people have gathered, learned, and grown for generations. You call it sentimental, but I call it irreplaceable."

The mayor sighed, spreading his hands. "I respect your passion, Mrs. Pearlson, truly. But the reality is that the library is underutilized. Its circulation numbers have declined steadily over the years, and foot traffic is at an all-time low. We simply cannot afford to keep it open."

Ella couldn't stay silent any longer. She shot to her feet, her voice trembling but determined. "That's because no one knows what's at stake! You're closing it without giving anyone a chance to fight for it."

The mayor looked at her, his brow furrowing slightly. "Miss Carter, I understand your concern, but the council has spent months reviewing this decision. The numbers don't lie."

"Numbers don't tell the whole story," Ella argued, her voice growing stronger. "This library isn't just about books. It's about people—about memories and history and everything this town is supposed to stand for."

A few people in the crowd nodded, but the majority remained silent, their faces unreadable. Ella glanced around, frustration boiling in her chest. Why weren't they angry? Why weren't they fighting back?

The mayor's tone softened slightly, as if speaking to a child. "I admire your passion, but passion alone won't pay the bills. The sale is final. The library will close in three weeks."

Ella sank back into her seat, her mind racing. Three weeks. That was all the time they had left. Around her, the crowd began to disperse, people murmuring to each other as they filed out of the room. Some looked resigned, others indifferent.

"How can they just accept this?" Ella muttered, her hands clenched into fists.

"Because they've forgotten what it means to fight for something they believe in," Mrs. Pearlson said quietly. "But you haven't. And neither have I."

Ella looked at the librarian, a spark of determination flaring in her chest. She wouldn't let this happen. She couldn't. The library wasn't just a relic of the past—it was the soul of Blythewood, and she was going to make sure everyone remembered that.

Ella sat cross-legged on the floor of her living room, the worn leather-bound book open in front of her. The map stared back at her, its delicate lines and mysterious symbols pulsing with the promise of secrets waiting to be uncovered. Around her, the chatter of her friends filled the room. Max was sprawled out on the couch, flipping a rubber band between his fingers like a slingshot. Jada sat cross-legged in an armchair, her tablet balanced on her knees, while Noah leaned against the wall, arms crossed, watching with quiet intensity.

"So, let me get this straight," Max said, pointing the rubber band at Ella like a weapon. "You're telling me you found a hidden book in the library, and it just so happens to contain a magical map? Are we living in a movie now?"

"It's not magical," Ella replied, rolling her eyes. "At least, I don't think it is. But it's definitely something important. Look at it!" She gestured at the map, her voice rising with excitement.

"It's hand-drawn, and the symbols are all over the library. Don't you think it's worth exploring?"

Jada leaned forward, pushing her glasses up the bridge of her nose as she studied the map. "It does look… intricate," she admitted. "Whoever made this took their time. These symbols aren't random—they're precise."

"Exactly," Ella said, her heart quickening. "Mrs. Pearlson told me about Evelyn Blythe—the woman who founded the library. She believed the library had a soul, that it held secrets. What if this map is one of them?"

Noah shifted his weight, his brow furrowing. "And what exactly are you hoping to find? Treasure? A hidden room full of gold?"

"I don't know," Ella admitted, looking up at him. "But with the library closing in three weeks, this could be our only chance to find out. What if it's something that could help us save it?"

Noah didn't respond immediately. He crouched down beside her, his practical nature kicking in as he studied the map. "It's definitely old," he said, tracing the edge of one of the symbols. "These marks here—they're not just decoration. They're pointing to something specific."

"See? Even Noah thinks it's worth a shot," Ella said, a triumphant smile spreading across her face.

"I didn't say that," Noah replied, though a small smirk tugged at his lips. "But I'll admit, it's interesting."

Max swung his legs off the couch, sitting upright for the first time. "Alright, I'm in," he declared, grinning. "If this leads to secret tunnels or pirate treasure, count me in. Plus, if we're sneaking around the library, I'm your guy. I've got stealth skills."

"No, you don't," Jada said flatly, not looking up from the tablet where she had started sketching a digital replica of the map. "You're loud and clumsy."

"Excuse me," Max shot back, clutching his chest dramatically. "I am graceful as a gazelle."

"You're as subtle as a bull in a china shop," Noah muttered, earning a snort from Jada.

"Focus, guys," Ella interrupted, though she couldn't hide her grin. "This is serious. If we're going to do this, we need a plan."

"Starting with what?" Max asked, leaning forward with exaggerated intensity. "The map says, 'Follow the symbols.' What does that even mean?"

"It means we start here," Ella said, pointing to the largest symbol on the map. It was a star, drawn over the biography section of the library. "This is where I found the book. It has to mean something."

Jada tilted her head, studying the symbol. "That's a good place to start. I can bring my tablet to document everything we find. If this map is part of something bigger, we'll need records."

"I'll bring my tools," Noah said, already thinking ahead. "If there's anything hidden—loose panels, secret compartments—I'll find it."

"And I'll bring snacks," Max chimed in, earning a collective groan from the others. "What? Every great adventure needs snacks."

"This isn't a picnic, Max," Ella said, shaking her head. "We're trying to save the library."

"I know," Max replied, his tone unusually serious. "That's why I'm in. The library's important—to all of us."

For a moment, the room fell quiet. Ella looked around at her friends, feeling a swell of gratitude. They didn't have to help her, but they were here anyway, ready to dive into the unknown.

"Thank you," she said softly, her voice thick with emotion. "I know this sounds crazy, but I really think this map could lead to something that changes everything."

"We've done crazier things," Jada said with a small smile. "Remember the treehouse project?"

Noah groaned. "Don't remind me. I'm still finding splinters from that."

Ella laughed, the tension in her chest easing. "Alright, then. Tomorrow, after school, we meet at the library. Bring whatever you need."

"Flashlights?" Max suggested.

"Sure," Ella said, standing up and closing the book carefully. "Flashlights, tools, snacks—whatever it takes. We're going to figure this out."

Max pumped his fist in the air. "Team Map is officially on the case!"

"Don't call us that," Jada muttered, but the corners of her mouth twitched upward.

As they packed up and headed out, Ella clutched the book tightly to her chest. For the first time since the council's announcement, she felt a flicker of hope. The library wasn't just a place. It was a puzzle, a mystery—and she wasn't going to let it disappear without a fight. With her friends by her side, she was ready to uncover whatever secrets it had been hiding.

The library was eerily quiet as the group gathered in the dimly lit biography section. Max juggled a flashlight between his hands, his expression a mix of boredom and curiosity. Jada sat cross-legged on the floor with her tablet balanced on her lap, scrolling through scanned pages of the map. Noah leaned against a nearby bookshelf, fiddling with a multi-tool, while Ella stood over the opened leather-bound book, her brow furrowed in concentration.

"This doesn't make any sense," Max said, breaking the silence. He flicked the flashlight on and off, casting erratic beams across the floor. "We've been staring at this thing for hours. Maybe it's just a bunch of doodles."

"They're not doodles," Ella snapped, her frustration bubbling over. She pointed at the intricate lines and symbols on the map. "Look at the detail. Someone went to a lot of trouble to draw this. It means something."

Jada adjusted her glasses, zooming in on the map's scanned image. "She's right. These markings are too precise to be random. But the problem is, they don't match anything I've found in the library's floor plans. It's like part of the building is... missing."

"Missing?" Noah asked, straightening. "What do you mean?"

"I mean the library's layout has changed over time," Jada explained, her tone patient. "Renovations, additions—it's not the same as when it was first built. If this map is from Evelyn Blythe's era, it might be pointing to something that doesn't exist anymore."

"Great," Max muttered, slumping against a bookshelf. "So we're chasing ghosts."

Ella shot him a glare. "You're not helping, Max."

"I'm just saying!" Max threw up his hands. "We're running around in circles, and all we've got to show for it is a headache."

"Maybe we're looking at it wrong," Noah said, his voice calm but firm. He knelt beside Ella and tapped the book. "What about these notes in the margins? They're in the same handwriting as the map. Maybe they're instructions."

Ella glanced at the notes, her frustration easing slightly. "They're cryptic, though. Look—'where stories begin' and 'under the watcher's gaze.' What does that even mean?"

"It's like a riddle," Jada murmured, leaning closer. "A lot of old maps have them. They're meant to guide you, but they're not straightforward."

"Well, that's just fantastic," Max said, crossing his arms. "I failed riddles in elementary school. What's next? We solve this and find out there's a pop quiz?"

"Max, could you maybe not talk for five minutes?" Ella said, her voice tight. She rubbed her temples, trying to focus. "We have to think. If Mrs. Blythe left this map, she wouldn't make it impossible to figure out. It has to connect to the library somehow."

"Wait," Noah said suddenly, his eyes narrowing. "You said, 'under the watcher's gaze.' What if that means something here? Like a statue or a portrait?"

Ella perked up. "There's a painting of Evelyn Blythe in the reading room. It's huge. She's sitting at a desk, looking right at you."

"That's worth checking out," Jada agreed, saving the map image to her tablet. "It could be a clue."

The group shuffled to the reading room, their footsteps echoing in the empty library. The large oil painting of Evelyn Blythe dominated the far wall, her stern yet kind gaze fixed on the room. Max stared up at it, tilting his head.

"She's kind of creepy," he said. "Like, in an old-school principal way."

"Focus, Max," Noah said, scanning the area beneath the painting. "If there's something here, it'll be close."

Ella crouched beside the desk in front of the painting, running her hands along its edges. The wood was smooth and polished, but one corner caught her attention. It felt uneven, as if it had been tampered with.

"Guys," she said, her voice hushed. "I think there's something here."

Jada knelt beside her, holding up the flashlight. "What is it?"

"This corner—it's loose." Ella pulled gently, and the piece of wood shifted, revealing a small compartment underneath. Inside was a folded piece of paper, yellowed with age.

"Please tell me that's not another map," Max groaned.

Ella unfolded the paper carefully, her eyes scanning the faded ink. "It's not a map. It's… instructions. It says, 'The heart of the library lies where the words have lived longest. Seek the first story.'"

"The first story?" Jada repeated. "What does that mean?"

"It's a metaphor," Noah said, his expression thoughtful. "The first story could mean the oldest book in the library. Maybe something in the rare books section?"

"Or it could be literal," Ella said, her excitement building. "The first story told in this library. Mrs. Blythe used to read to kids when it first opened. Maybe there's a connection."

"That narrows it down to… everything," Max said, waving his hands. "Fantastic."

"No, it's a start," Ella said, her voice firm. "This proves we're on the right track. There's something here, something Mrs. Blythe wanted us to find. We just have to keep looking."

Despite their frustration, Ella saw the determination in her friends' faces. They were in this together, and they weren't going to give up. She folded the instructions and slipped them into her pocket, her resolve strengthening.

"Alright," Ella said, standing up. "Tomorrow, we hit the rare books section. We're going to figure this out, piece by piece."

Max sighed dramatically but gave a mock salute. "Yes, Captain Ella. Lead us to glory."

Jada smirked. "Or at least to some answers."

As they filed out of the reading room, Ella couldn't shake the feeling that they were close—closer than they realized—to uncovering the library's secrets.

Chapter 4
Secrets in the Shelves

The morning light streamed through the library's stained-glass windows, casting slivers of vibrant color across the floor. It was early—too early for the library to be officially open—but Mrs. Pearlson had let them in with little more than a knowing nod and a quiet "Don't break anything, children." Now, the soft sounds of footsteps and whispered voices filled the air as Ella, Max, Jada, and Noah gathered in the biography section.

Ella crouched on the floor, the map spread carefully across the base of one of the shelves. She traced a faint, swirling star symbol near the center of the map with her finger, her brow furrowed in concentration. "This is it," she said finally, looking up at the others. "The next mark."

"The biography section?" Max asked, his tone skeptical as he glanced at the rows of dusty books. "Seems a little obvious, doesn't it?"

"It's not about obvious," Jada chimed in, her tablet already out as she zoomed in on the digital version of the map. "It's about *where* in the biography section. That star wouldn't be here if there wasn't something special."

Noah knelt beside Ella, squinting at the map's faint details. "The symbol's right against the wall," he muttered, his fingers brushing the map before turning toward the towering shelves. "That wall."

Max spun on his heel to face it, his grin already forming. "Hidden compartments and mysterious walls? Now *we're* talking." He stepped forward, running his hands along the spines of the old books before pressing his palm flat against the wood paneling. "Alright, library, show me your secrets."

"Max, don't—" Noah started, but it was already too late.

Max pushed harder against the panel near the shelf's edge, and with a muffled creak, the wood gave a fraction of an inch. A deep, hollow sound echoed in response.

The group froze.

Jada's voice was barely a whisper. "Did you hear that?"

"Uh, yeah." Max's grin grew wider as he turned back to Noah. "That's the sound of me being *awesome.*"

Noah shot him a glare before leaning in closer, his hands now carefully examining the same spot. "There's a gap," he said quietly, pressing his fingers against the uneven edge. "It's not part of the shelf. It's a panel—probably built into the wall itself."

Ella's pulse quickened as she stood up, hovering anxiously behind them. "You mean it's a hidden door?"

"More like a hidden compartment," Noah replied, glancing back at her. "Whatever's behind this, someone went through a lot of trouble to hide it."

Max cracked his knuckles, clearly relishing the moment. "Well, lucky for us, I've got magic hands."

"Just don't break it," Ella warned, though her voice trembled with excitement.

"I'm not going to break it," Max replied confidently, gripping the edge of the panel. "I'm going to reveal its secrets."

With one final shove, the wood shifted further, and a low, echoing *click* filled the air. A section of the wall, no wider than a doorframe, groaned as it slowly swung inward. Dust billowed out in a cloud, making them all cough and wave their hands in front of their faces.

"Max, I swear—" Jada started, but her voice trailed off as the dust settled and the hidden compartment revealed itself.

It wasn't a compartment at all. It was a vault.

The space behind the wall was small and dark, no more than a shallow recess hidden between two sets of shelves. Against the back wall sat an ornate, wrought-iron door, its surface covered in delicate engravings that twisted and swirled like vines growing around a garden gate. The metal was old but sturdy, and though the lock appeared rusted, it still glinted faintly in the filtered light.

Ella stared, breathless. "It's a vault," she whispered.

Max let out a triumphant laugh. "I *told* you something was here! Who's the genius now?"

Noah ignored him, stepping closer to the vault door with cautious curiosity. "This isn't just any old hiding spot. Look at the design—it's deliberate. Someone put this here for a reason."

Jada took a step forward, tilting her head as she studied the engravings. "It's beautiful. Like… something out of a fairy tale."

Ella swallowed hard, her voice soft. "It has to be Mrs. Blythe. She built this library to last. She must have hidden something important here."

Max, ever impatient, grabbed the handle of the door and tugged. It didn't budge. He frowned, pulling harder. "Of course it's locked. Because why make it easy?"

"Let me see," Noah said, moving Max aside. He crouched down, inspecting the lock with quiet focus. "It's old but not broken. I might be able to open it… if we had the right key."

"A key?" Jada echoed, glancing between them. "We don't have a key."

"Not yet," Noah replied, standing up. "But if Mrs. Blythe hid this vault, she hid the key somewhere too. Maybe the map will tell us."

Max groaned, slumping dramatically against the wall. "Great. So we found the vault, but we can't even open it?"

Ella's mind raced, her eyes fixed on the intricate door. "This isn't the end, Max. It's a step forward. We found something—something no one else knows about. That means we're on the right path."

Noah nodded, his gaze serious. "We'll figure this out. We always do."

"Yeah," Max said reluctantly, though his grin returned quickly. "And when we do, I'm calling dibs on whatever's behind that door."

"Unless it's cursed," Jada muttered, smirking as she tucked her tablet under her arm.

Ella looked at her friends, her heart pounding with anticipation. This was more than a clue—more than just a dusty map and old words. The vault was real, and so was the mystery.

"Let's go," she said softly. "We'll come back for this."

As they stepped away, leaving the vault concealed behind its hidden panel once more, Ella glanced over her shoulder, that faint scent of lavender brushing past her like a whisper.

The library wasn't done with them yet.

The vault door creaked open slowly, its hinges groaning under decades of neglect. A thin cloud of dust spilled out, swirling lazily in the slivers of light that snuck through the cracks of the hidden wall. Ella stepped inside first, her breath catching as her eyes adjusted to the dim interior.

The space was small—barely large enough to hold them all—but what it held was extraordinary. Rows of shelves, smaller and more delicate than those outside, lined the walls, each cradling books that looked older than the library itself. Their covers were faded, their edges worn, but there was something almost alive about them, as though they had been waiting for someone to find them.

"Whoa..." Max's voice broke the silence as he stepped in behind her. He stared at the shelves, his eyes wide with wonder. "Is this... is this a *treasure room* for books?"

"Looks like it," Noah murmured, following close behind. His gaze swept the shelves carefully, taking in the leather-bound spines and gold-embossed titles. "These aren't just old books. These are first editions."

Jada squeezed through the doorway last, her tablet clutched to her chest. She turned a slow circle, her mouth slightly open. "I've never seen anything like this. Look at the craftsmanship... the bindings, the lettering. These are priceless."

Ella knelt carefully beside the nearest shelf, her hands trembling slightly as she reached for a book. Its spine was cracked but still elegant, the title barely readable: *The Collected Works of Jane Eyre.*

When she opened it, the first page revealed an inscription written in looping cursive:

"To the Blythewood Library—may its walls always hold stories worth telling."

She swallowed, her voice soft. "Look at this."

Noah crouched beside her, peering over her shoulder. His brow furrowed as he read the inscription aloud. "'May its walls always hold stories worth telling.' Someone dedicated this book to the library."

Jada moved to another shelf, pulling a thinner volume free. "Here's another one," she said, flipping it open. Her voice was quiet but steady. "'To the children who find solace in words, may these pages be your refuge.'"

Max whistled, bending low to look at the rows of books stacked carefully together. "These are like… messages. Little time capsules from people who cared about this place." He picked up a worn hardcover with faded gilding. "This one says, 'For those who dream beyond these walls—keep dreaming.'"

Ella stood slowly, her heart pounding in her chest. "These aren't just books. They're stories. Pieces of people's lives that were left here."

Noah nodded, carefully sliding a thin, blue book back into its place. "Each one has a dedication. That's why Mrs. Blythe kept them hidden. She knew how important they were."

"And how valuable," Jada added, her voice tinged with awe. "These are first editions, Ella. If the town knew about this… if the council knew… it could change everything."

Max's face lit up, his grin triumphant. "You're saying these dusty old books could save the library?"

"Yes," Ella said, her voice firm. "This is what we've been looking for. Proof that this library isn't just some building. It's part of the town's history, its *soul*."

Jada looked up from a particularly fragile book, her fingers careful as she turned its pages. "If we show the council what's here, they won't be able to ignore it. They'd have to realize what they're about to destroy."

"But we have to be careful," Noah interjected, his gaze serious as it swept the vault. "If people find out too soon, the wrong person might take these books for themselves. Something this valuable doesn't stay secret for long."

Ella nodded. "We'll document everything first. Jada, can you start cataloging the books? Photos, titles, inscriptions—everything."

Jada perked up instantly, pulling her tablet closer. "Already on it. I'll back everything up tonight. By the time we're done, we'll have a full record of every book here."

Max clapped his hands together, startling them all. "This is it, guys. We found the library's treasure. Mrs. Blythe totally knew what she was doing." He paused, grinning at Ella. "You were right, Captain Carter. We're going to save this place."

Ella smiled, the weight of doubt finally lifting off her shoulders. For weeks, the library had felt like a fragile thing—slipping through her fingers no matter how tightly she held on. But now, standing in this secret vault surrounded by stories and whispered dedications, she felt something else entirely: hope.

"This isn't just about saving the library," she said softly, her gaze sweeping the shelves. "It's about honoring the people who came before us. The ones who believed in this place."

"And making sure everyone else does too," Noah added, rising to his feet. "We need to get this right. These books deserve to be seen."

Max grinned, hoisting his backpack higher on his shoulder. "And when we're done, they'll build a statue of us in the square. Heroes of Blythewood Library."

Jada snorted, not looking up from her tablet. "Don't hold your breath."

Ella chuckled, but her smile didn't fade. She let her fingers trail along one of the spines, feeling the texture of the worn leather. "We're not done yet. This is only the beginning."

They turned one last time to look at the vault before carefully pulling the door closed, sealing the books—and their secrets— away again. As they stepped back into the library's main hall, the faint scent of lavender drifted through the air, as if someone were watching, proud and patient.

"Thank you, Mrs. Blythe," Ella whispered to herself.

The library still had stories to tell, and they were the ones who would bring them to life.

Ella sat cross-legged on the carpeted floor of the library, the soft hum of silence enveloping her. One of the books from the vault rested in her lap, its cracked leather spine fragile beneath her hands. Sunlight filtered faintly through the tall windows, casting faint patterns of gold on the biography shelves, but Ella wasn't paying attention to the light. Her gaze was fixed on the words inscribed inside the front cover:

"To Blythewood Library—where every reader finds a home."

The words tugged at something deep inside her. It was more than just ink on paper. It was a promise, a reminder of what the library stood for. She traced the faded letters gently, as if touching them would make their meaning clearer.

Max sprawled out beside her, his head propped up on one hand as he absentmindedly flipped through another of the vault's books. "I still can't believe this was hidden in the wall. A treasure trove of old books, just sitting there."

"Waiting to be found," Ella murmured, still staring at the dedication.

Noah leaned against a nearby shelf, his arms crossed. "It's incredible, sure, but we can't just sit on this forever. These books won't mean anything if we don't do something with them."

"I know." Ella looked up at him, her fingers tapping softly on the cover. "I just…" She hesitated, chewing her bottom lip as an idea began to take root, growing stronger with each second. "What if we *show* everyone?"

Jada, perched on the edge of a chair with her tablet balanced on her knees, looked up. "Show them?"

Ella's eyes brightened. "Yeah. I mean, think about it. What if we host an event—something at the library—where we showcase these books? People could come see them, learn their history, and understand why they matter. Why *the library* matters."

Max sat up, suddenly interested. "Like a… book exhibit?"

"No, more than that," Ella said, her excitement building. She pushed the book aside and gestured as she spoke, her hands framing the air like she was already seeing it come together. "A literary event. We'll display the books, read some of the dedications aloud, share the stories of how this library changed people's lives. It'll be a way to remind everyone what we stand to lose if it's sold."

Jada's brows lifted as she considered it, her fingers poised over her tablet. "That's… actually a really good idea. A community event would get people's attention. If we tie it to the history of the library and these books, it might get the town council to listen."

"Exactly," Ella said, her voice stronger now. "These books aren't just artifacts. They're proof. Proof that this library has been a home for so many people. If we can show that history, we can make them *care*."

Noah, ever practical, frowned slightly as he spoke. "And how are we going to pull that off? This isn't some small classroom project. We'd need people to show up. We'd need displays, readers—something that feels *big*."

"We'll figure it out," Ella replied, meeting his gaze. "We have time. If we work together, we can make it happen."

Max clapped his hands together, breaking the momentary silence. "I love it. A secret vault of books turning into a full-blown literary festival? This is some movie-level stuff right here." He paused, grinning. "Can I emcee? I'd make an excellent host."

Jada snorted. "You'd turn it into a comedy show."

"Exactly," Max shot back, winking. "It'll keep people entertained."

Noah sighed but didn't look unconvinced. "If we're going to do this, we need a plan. We can't wing it, not if we want people to take it seriously."

"I'll work on the logistics," Jada said, her fingers already flying across her tablet screen as she made notes. "We'll need flyers, announcements—something to spread the word. And we'll have to involve Mrs. Pearlson."

"She'll help," Ella said confidently. "She wants to save the library as much as we do."

Noah tilted his head slightly, his tone softening. "You really believe this will work, don't you?"

"I do," Ella said, the words coming out steady and sure. "Because it has to. The library isn't just a building. It's a home for stories—for memories—and for people like us who find something here they can't find anywhere else."

Max grinned, nudging her shoulder lightly. "Well, I'm all in. Operation Save the Library just got its game plan."

Jada smiled faintly, glancing up from her tablet. "Count me in too. If we're doing this, we're doing it right."

Noah's gaze lingered on the rows of shelves, his brow furrowed as if still weighing the possibilities. Finally, he gave a small nod. "Alright. I'm in. But we'll need to move fast."

Ella picked up the book in her lap once more, its dedication catching the fading light. A glimmer of hope warmed her chest as she stood, clutching it tightly. "Then let's get started."

The library seemed to hum softly around them, as if it had heard their plan and approved. This wasn't just a fight to save a building. It was a fight to save stories—stories like these, which had been hidden for so long but were finally ready to be shared.

For the first time, the path ahead felt clear, and Ella knew, deep in her bones, that they could do this. The library's stories weren't finished yet—and neither was she.

Chapter 5
The Vault Revealed

The biography section of the library was darker than usual, the overhead lights casting long shadows between the towering shelves. Ella stood at the map's starting point, her flashlight beam steady as it illuminated the shelves. The air smelled of old paper and wood polish, and the weight of their mission hung heavily in the silence.

"Okay," Ella said, her voice hushed. "The map says the next clue is here, but we've combed through this section twice already. There has to be something we're missing."

"Define 'missing,'" Max said, leaning against a nearby shelf and flicking his flashlight toward the ceiling. "Because all I see are books. Lots and lots of dusty, boring books."

"It's not the books," Jada interjected, crouching by the base of the shelf. Her tablet glowed faintly as she compared the map's symbols to the surrounding area. "It's something else. Something hidden. Look—this marking here on the map." She pointed to a small star etched near the corner of the section. "It lines up with this shelf."

"Hidden treasures in the library," Max muttered, pushing off the shelf. "Sounds like a bedtime story."

"Or reality," Noah said, kneeling beside Jada. His voice was calm, but his eyes were sharp with focus. "Maps don't lie, Max. Someone put this here for a reason."

Max crossed his arms. "Or maybe someone just wanted to mess with us."

Ella shot him a look. "Can you try being useful for once?"

"Fine, fine," Max said, throwing up his hands. "What do you want me to do? Start pulling random books off the shelf like in the movies?"

"That's actually not a bad idea," Noah said, standing up and brushing dust off his jeans. "Sometimes hidden mechanisms are disguised as ordinary things. Let's give it a try."

The group exchanged glances before fanning out along the shelf. Each of them began testing books, tugging gently on their spines, while Ella kept the flashlight steady. The room was filled with the soft sound of shuffling books and the occasional thud of displaced dust.

"This feels ridiculous," Max said, pulling a particularly thick volume with an exaggerated flourish. "If I find a secret door, I'm officially demanding we rename the library after me."

"You won't," Jada replied without looking up from her tablet. "Because you're not pulling the right books."

"Oh, and you are?" Max retorted, leaning on a shelf.

"Guys," Ella said, her voice sharp. "Focus."

It was Noah who paused first. His fingers had brushed against something unusual near the middle of the shelf—an edge that felt too smooth, too perfect compared to the rest of the wood. He froze, running his fingers over the area again.

"Ella," he said quietly. "I think I've got something."

The room fell silent as everyone turned to him. Ella stepped closer, shining her flashlight over his hand. There, barely visible beneath the rows of books, was a faint seam running horizontally along the shelf.

"What is that?" Jada asked, peering over Ella's shoulder.

"A panel," Noah said, his voice steady. "It's flush with the wood, but it's definitely separate. And look—" He pointed to a small groove near the bottom corner. "That's not a design flaw. It's a latch."

"Finally!" Max said, practically bouncing on his toes. "Our hidden treasure awaits."

"Or it's just a compartment full of old papers," Jada said skeptically, but there was a flicker of curiosity in her tone.

Noah didn't respond. He slid his multi-tool from his pocket and carefully inserted the edge into the groove. The others watched in tense silence as he worked the tool, his hands steady and deliberate. With a faint *click*, the panel shifted slightly, a puff of dust escaping from the seam.

"There," Noah said, exhaling. "It's loose."

"Open it," Ella urged, her voice barely above a whisper.

Noah pushed the panel gently, and it swung inward, revealing a dark recess behind it. The air that escaped was cool and musty, carrying the scent of something long forgotten. Ella crouched beside him, shining her flashlight into the opening.

Inside was a small wooden handle attached to what appeared to be a lever.

"Are we sure we want to pull that?" Jada asked, eyeing the lever warily. "What if it sets off an alarm? Or collapses the shelf?"

"Only one way to find out," Max said, reaching toward the lever.

"Don't touch it!" Ella hissed, swatting his hand away. She turned to Noah. "You found it. It's your call."

Noah hesitated for a moment, his brow furrowed. Then he nodded, gripping the handle firmly. "Here goes nothing."

With a smooth, deliberate motion, he pulled the lever. For a moment, nothing happened. Then, with a low groan, the section of the bookshelf directly to their left began to shift. The sound of grinding wood and metal filled the room as the shelf slid outward, revealing a narrow doorway hidden behind it.

The group stared in stunned silence.

"Okay," Max said finally, his voice filled with awe. "That… was cool."

Ella stepped forward, her flashlight beam slicing through the dust-filled air beyond the doorway. The space beyond was dark, but the faint outline of stone walls was visible.

"Is that…?" Jada began, trailing off.

"A hidden room," Ella finished, her voice trembling with a mix of excitement and disbelief. "This is it. This is what the map was pointing to."

They stood there for a moment, taking in the gravity of their discovery. The air was thick with the weight of history, untouched for decades. Ella felt a shiver run down her spine. Whatever lay ahead, she knew it would change everything.

The hidden door creaked as Ella pushed it open, the sound echoing faintly in the darkness beyond. Dust swirled in the beam of her flashlight, and the air was cooler here, carrying the unmistakable scent of time and decay. She stepped forward cautiously, her breath catching as the flashlight revealed rows of shelves lined with books.

"Whoa," Max whispered, stepping in behind her. His usual sarcastic tone was replaced by genuine awe. "This is… incredible."

The room was smaller than Ella had imagined, its stone walls curving slightly inward as if the space had been carved out of the earth itself. The shelves were built into the walls, their wood darkened with age. Each book looked like a treasure, their spines bearing intricate designs, gold lettering, and colors dulled by time.

"Are these… rare books?" Jada asked, her voice hushed. She moved to one of the shelves, her fingers hovering above the tomes without touching them. "Some of these look ancient."

"They probably are," Noah said, shining his flashlight over the shelves. He crouched down, his eyes scanning the lower levels. "Look at the care that went into this. Whoever built this place wanted these books to last."

Ella stepped further in, her flashlight revealing more of the room. Each book was unique, some bound in leather, others in materials she couldn't even identify. She picked one up carefully, its cover embossed with a swirling gold pattern. Opening it, she gasped softly.

"Guys, look at this," she said, holding the book out to the group.

Jada leaned in, squinting at the inscription on the first page. "'To my dearest Ella Mae Carter, for the stories you'll one day tell.'" She blinked, looking at Ella. "That's… your grandmother's name."

Ella nodded, her throat tight. "This was hers. She must've donated it to the library. I had no idea."

"Check this one," Noah said, pulling another book from the shelf. "'To Marcus Thorne, whose courage inspired a town.'" He frowned. "These aren't just books. They're… dedications."

"It's like a time capsule," Jada said, her voice tinged with awe. "These books were left here by people who loved the library. They're part of its history."

Max ran his fingers along the spines of the books, his expression uncharacteristically solemn. "This is… kind of amazing," he admitted. "It's like the library kept these pieces of everyone who cared about it."

Ella set the book down carefully and moved further into the room, her flashlight catching something at the back of the vault. A small pedestal stood there, its surface covered by a thin layer of dust. Resting on top was a gold bookmark, its edges intricately engraved.

"What's this?" she murmured, reaching out to pick it up.

The group gathered around as she turned the bookmark over in her hands. Its surface gleamed in the light, and engraved along its length were the words: *Every story leads to another.*

"What does it mean?" Max asked, leaning in for a closer look.

"I think it's a clue," Ella said, her voice steady despite the rapid thudding of her heart. "Mrs. Blythe must've left this here for a reason. It has to be connected to the map."

"'Every story leads to another,'" Jada repeated thoughtfully. "It's poetic, but it's also literal, isn't it? Stories do lead to other stories—books reference each other, histories connect…"

"And maps," Noah added, glancing at Ella. "This bookmark is pointing us to the next part of the puzzle."

Ella nodded, her excitement growing. "The map didn't stop with the hidden door. It has more symbols, more places to search. This bookmark is telling us to keep going."

Max let out a low whistle. "So, we're on some kind of epic scavenger hunt now? What's next, buried treasure?"

"Maybe," Ella said, her voice tinged with both determination and wonder. "Or maybe something even better. If these books are anything to go by, whatever we find next will be just as important."

Jada was already scanning the shelves with her tablet, documenting the titles and inscriptions. "We need to catalog everything here. This is too important to keep hidden. These books could prove the library's value—not just as a place for borrowing books, but as a repository for the town's history."

"Agreed," Noah said, his tone resolute. "But we have to be careful. If word gets out about this place, it could be compromised. The developers—or anyone, really—might not respect its significance."

Ella looked around the room, her chest tight with a mix of pride and fear. This vault was a treasure, a tangible reminder of what the library meant to Blythewood. And now, they were the ones tasked with protecting it.

She held up the bookmark, the words gleaming in the flashlight's beam. "This is our next step," she said firmly. "We follow the map, figure out what Mrs. Blythe was trying to show us. But we do it quietly. No one can know about this. Not yet."

"Agreed," Noah said, nodding.

"Fine," Max added, though his grin betrayed his excitement. "But when we find the next clue, I call dibs on the dramatic reveal."

Jada rolled her eyes. "You can have your dramatic moment, Max. Just don't drop anything."

As the group began to pack up, carefully placing the books back where they found them, Ella took one last look at the vault. This wasn't just about saving the library anymore. It was about uncovering the legacy it had preserved—and making sure that legacy lived on.

The group huddled in the center of the vault, their flashlights casting uneven beams of light that bounced off the dusty shelves and stone walls. The air felt heavier now, charged with the weight of what they had uncovered. Ella stood with the gold bookmark in her hand, her mind racing as she looked at the shelves around them. The dedications in the books spoke volumes about the library's importance to the town's history and its people. But the question hanging in the air was: what would they do now?

"This vault," Jada began, her voice quiet but steady, "it's not just a collection of old books. It's a record of the town's soul. Every person who left a book here left a piece of themselves, of their story."

"That's exactly why it has to stay hidden," Noah said, leaning against a shelf with his arms crossed. His usual calm demeanor was tinged with unease. "If the wrong people find out about this, it'll be exploited. Developers won't care about the history—they'll see dollar signs."

"Then what are we supposed to do?" Max asked, sitting cross-legged on the floor. He spun his flashlight idly, the beam flickering across the walls. "Keep it a secret forever? That doesn't exactly help us save the library."

Ella turned to face them, her fingers gripping the bookmark tightly. "We can't keep this a secret," she said firmly. "This vault proves the library's worth. It's the kind of evidence the council can't ignore."

"And how do we show it to them without tipping off the developers?" Noah countered, his tone challenging but not unkind. "If they find out about this, they'll find a way to spin it. They'll argue that the books could be moved to a museum or a private collection. The library wouldn't matter to them anymore."

Jada frowned, her tablet balanced on her lap as she scrolled through the photos she had taken of the inscriptions. "Noah has a point. We need to be strategic. If we just present this without context, we could lose control of the narrative."

Ella exhaled sharply, pacing a small circle in the center of the room. The weight of the situation pressed down on her shoulders, but she refused to let it crush her. "So, we control the narrative," she said, her voice gaining strength. "We don't just show them the books. We show them what they mean—what this vault means."

"Easier said than done," Max muttered, leaning back on his elbows. "You're talking about convincing a bunch of politicians and developers that this dusty room is worth more than whatever millions they're being offered."

"Not just politicians," Jada said, her tone thoughtful. "The town. If we can get the community to rally around the library, the council will have to listen. They won't be able to ignore public opinion."

Max snorted. "Yeah, because everyone in this town is just itching to fight for a library they haven't set foot in for years."

"Maybe they haven't fought for it because they didn't know what they were losing," Ella shot back, her eyes flashing. "If they see this—if they understand what's at stake—they'll care. I know they will."

Noah stepped forward, his gaze steady. "But we need a plan. Something airtight. If we rush into this, we risk losing everything."

Ella nodded, her frustration giving way to determination. "You're right. We have to be smart about this. We'll document everything—photos, videos, detailed notes. Jada, you're in charge of organizing it all."

Jada nodded, her fingers already flying across her tablet screen. "I can put together a digital presentation. Something that tells the story of the vault and the people who contributed to it."

"Noah," Ella continued, turning to him, "you'll help me figure out how to present this to the council. We need to anticipate their arguments and be ready to counter them."

"Got it," Noah said simply.

"And me?" Max asked, raising a hand lazily. "What's my job in this master plan?"

Ella hesitated for a moment before smirking. "You're our public relations guy."

Max sat up, feigning offense. "Public relations? What, you mean I'm the face of this operation?"

"You're good with people," Jada said, not looking up from her screen. "You can talk to them without making them want to run in the opposite direction. Most of the time."

Max grinned, taking the jab in stride. "Fine. I'll charm the socks off this town. You'll see."

As the group settled into their roles, the gravity of the situation began to sink in. The vault wasn't just a discovery—it was a responsibility. They were the only ones who knew about it, and the only ones who could protect it. Ella felt a flicker of fear in her chest, but she quickly pushed it aside. There was no room for doubt. Not now.

Jada looked up from her tablet, her expression serious. "We need to be careful. If word gets out before we're ready, it could backfire."

"We won't let that happen," Ella said firmly. "We'll move quickly, but we'll be smart about it. No one outside this group knows about the vault until we're ready."

"Fine by me," Noah said. "But we should get moving. The longer we stay here, the more likely someone will notice something's up."

Ella nodded, slipping the gold bookmark into her bag. She took one last look around the vault, her heart swelling with a mix of pride and resolve. This was their fight now, and they weren't going to back down.

"Let's get to work," she said, leading the group out of the hidden room and back into the library's quiet halls. The stakes had never been higher, but for the first time, Ella felt ready to face them head-on.

Chapter 6
Every Story Leads to Another

The town hall felt colder than usual, its high ceilings amplifying every sound, every footstep, like echoes in a cavern. Ella gripped the notebook in her hands so tightly the corners curled. She glanced at her friends—Max, Jada, and Noah—standing just behind her like a wall of quiet support. Max wore his usual grin, but it was thinner this time, stretched over his nerves. Jada stood tall, her tablet tucked under her arm, determination etched across her face. Noah's expression was calm, though his hands flexed at his sides like he was bracing for something.

Across the room, Mayor Grayson sat behind his oversized desk, his expression unreadable as he regarded them. The polished wood of the desk gleamed under the fluorescent lights, papers stacked neatly as though nothing could ever disturb his ordered world.

"Ella Carter," the mayor said finally, his tone polite but clipped. "What can I do for you and… your team this afternoon?"

"We have something to show you, Mr. Grayson," Ella began, forcing her voice to sound steady. "Something important."

The mayor raised an eyebrow, folding his hands in front of him. "I see."

Jada stepped forward, setting her tablet on the desk and swiping quickly to pull up the photos of the letters and bookmarks. "We found these in the library," she explained, her voice firm.

"Letters. Bookmarks. Messages left behind by people who were helped by the library—people whose lives were changed by it."

"And rare first-edition books," Noah added, his voice low but resolute. "Books with dedications that prove the library is part of this town's history. You can't replace that."

The mayor's gaze flicked between them, his lips thinning slightly. "Is that so?" He leaned back in his chair, his expression as unyielding as stone. "You've been very busy, I see. But what exactly are you hoping to accomplish here?"

Ella stepped closer, holding up the notebook filled with transcribed dedications. "We're trying to show you why the library matters. These letters, these books—they're proof that it's more than just a building. It's part of the community. You can't sell something that means so much to so many people."

For a moment, Mayor Grayson said nothing. His gaze rested on the open tablet, the photos of the letters glowing faintly in the harsh light. Then he let out a slow breath and shook his head.

"Miss Carter," he said evenly, his voice devoid of warmth, "I understand your passion. I admire it, even. But you're asking me to put sentimentality above practicality. The library may have meant something once, but times have changed."

"It still means something!" Max cut in, unable to hold back. He stepped forward, jabbing a finger toward the photos. "Did you even read those? People depended on the library—people who had nothing else. Are you just going to ignore that?"

The mayor's expression hardened. "This isn't about ignoring anything. It's about moving forward. The town can't survive on memories alone, young man."

Jada's voice sharpened as she jumped in. "It's not just memories. It's history. And it's community. The library isn't holding this town back—it's part of what makes it worth saving."

Mayor Grayson sighed, pushing the tablet back across the desk. "You don't understand the decisions I have to make. Economic recovery requires sacrifice, and the library's land is valuable. We can't afford to be sentimental."

Ella's confidence wavered as his words hit her like cold water. *Sentimental.* He said it like it was a dirty word, like the lives they were fighting for didn't matter.

"But you're wrong," she said, her voice trembling just slightly. "This isn't just sentimentality. The library gives people hope. It's a safe place—a place that's helped more people than you realize. If you destroy it, you're destroying all of that."

The mayor's eyes narrowed slightly, though his tone remained calm. "And what do you suggest I do instead? Keep the library open out of nostalgia while the rest of the town struggles to stay afloat? Passion is admirable, Miss Carter, but passion doesn't pay bills."

Noah stepped up beside Ella, his voice low but cutting through the tension. "If you tear the library down, you're giving up on the people who believed in this town in the first place."

Mayor Grayson met his gaze, something flickering across his face—just for a moment—before it vanished. "I've heard enough," he said curtly, turning his attention back to Ella. "I appreciate what you're trying to do, but this matter has already been decided. The council will vote to finalize the sale at the end of the month."

"You're making a mistake," Ella said quietly, clutching the notebook against her chest like a shield. "You're choosing short-term gain over something that lasts."

The mayor stood then, signaling the end of the conversation. "Sometimes hard decisions have to be made. I'm sorry, Miss Carter, but the library will not save this town."

The room was silent as his words hung in the air like an unshakable wall. Ella felt her chest tighten, her confidence faltering as though the floor had been pulled out from under her.

Max broke the silence, his voice quieter than usual. "You're wrong." He pointed at the photos one last time. "One day, you'll see that."

"Come on," Noah said softly, putting a hand on Ella's shoulder as he guided her back toward the door.

Jada grabbed her tablet, shooting the mayor one last glare before following them. As the door clicked shut behind them, the cold weight of defeat settled over Ella like a shadow.

"Ella?" Max asked gently, his voice soft as they stepped out into the empty hallway.

Ella swallowed hard, looking down at the notebook in her hands. "He doesn't care," she whispered. "He's not going to listen."

Jada stopped beside her, frowning. "That doesn't mean we stop trying."

"He's just one person," Noah added, his tone firm. "The whole town hasn't seen what we've found yet. We'll show them. All of them."

Max gave a crooked smile, nudging Ella's arm. "Yeah, the mayor doesn't get the final say. The people do. And you're way tougher than he thinks you are."

Ella looked at her friends, their determination lighting up the quiet hallway. Slowly, she took a deep breath, forcing the weight of doubt back. "You're right," she said softly. "We'll show them. We're not done yet."

Ella sat cross-legged on her bed, the journal splayed open in front of her, its fragile pages glowing softly under the golden beam of her bedside lamp. Outside the window, the world had faded into a quiet, moonlit stillness. Inside, her room felt like a different kind of quiet—the heavy, suffocating kind that filled the spaces between her thoughts.

The mayor's words echoed over and over in her mind.

"Sentimental but impractical."
"Passion doesn't pay bills."
"The library will not save this town."

Ella's chest tightened as her eyes skimmed the familiar map drawn by Mrs. Blythe, the lines almost comforting now—the only thing that made sense. She traced one of the swirls with her fingertip, its curves delicate and careful. There was no hesitation in Mrs. Blythe's lines, no doubt in her words, and yet…

"Maybe he's right," Ella whispered to herself. The words sounded strange in the stillness, like they didn't belong to her. "What if this isn't enough?"

Her fingers brushed the handwritten message at the front of the journal, the one that had started all of this: *"To those who seek the library's soul, follow the map and you will find what has been hidden."*

But what had they really found? Old letters, dusty books, forgotten memories—beautiful, yes, but would any of it matter to people who cared about money more than history?

With a frustrated sigh, she shut the journal, the sound sharp in the silence. She buried her face in her hands, her thoughts spinning relentlessly. *We've tried so hard. What if it's not enough to change their minds? What if we lose?*

The door creaked softly as it opened, and Ella looked up just in time to see her mom step into the room, carrying a steaming mug.

"Hey, El." Her mom's voice was gentle, the way it always was when she could tell something was wrong. "You've been awfully quiet tonight."

Ella straightened, quickly wiping her face with the back of her hand. "I'm fine."

Her mom tilted her head, setting the mug—hot cocoa, by the smell of it—on the nightstand. "You don't look fine." She sat at the edge of the bed, her gaze kind but probing. "Want to tell me what's on your mind?"

For a moment, Ella didn't answer. She stared down at the journal in her lap, her fingers tracing its edge absentmindedly. "It's just… I'm trying to save something that no one else seems to care about."

Her mom raised an eyebrow. "The library?"

Ella nodded slowly. "We found these letters, Mom. And books with dedications—stories from people who came to the library when they had nowhere else to go. We've worked so hard to show why it matters, but the mayor—" Her voice faltered, bitterness seeping in. "He said it's all just sentimentality. That it doesn't matter because it won't fix the town's problems."

Her mom was quiet for a moment, studying her carefully. "And do you believe that?"

Ella hesitated. "I don't know," she admitted. "What if he's right? What if we're just wasting time?"

Her mom shook her head, reaching out to tuck a strand of hair behind Ella's ear like she used to when Ella was little. "Ella, the people who get remembered aren't the ones who sit quietly when something they love is at risk. They're the ones who fight, even when the odds seem impossible."

Ella blinked, her voice soft. "But what if we fail?"

Her mom smiled faintly. "Sometimes you have to fight anyway. Even if you're scared. Even if you don't know how it'll turn out. You're not just trying to save a building, El. You're trying to save what it *means* to people."

Ella looked down at the journal again, her mom's words settling over her like a steadying hand. She opened it carefully, flipping back to Mrs. Blythe's looping handwriting on the first page. The words felt different this time—stronger.

"Follow the map and you will find what has been hidden."

Her mom stood up, pressing a kiss to the top of Ella's head. "Don't give up on it, sweetheart. Sometimes, all it takes is one person to remind everyone else why something is worth saving."

Ella didn't answer right away, but after her mom left, she whispered into the quiet, "I'll try."

The journal sat open in her lap again, the map glowing faintly in the soft light. Ella let her fingers trail over its edges, feeling the weight of what it represented. Mrs. Blythe had believed in this library enough to protect its secrets, to leave behind something for someone like Ella to find.

She believed it was worth saving.

And maybe—just maybe—that was enough.

Ella sat at her desk, the soft glow of her lamp spilling light across the open journal in front of her. She had spent the last hour staring at the map, the words looping over and over in her mind. *"Follow the map and you will find what has been hidden."*

The weight of the mayor's dismissal still lingered like a shadow she couldn't shake. Every plan they'd made, every discovery they'd unearthed, felt suddenly fragile—like one sharp breath could blow it all apart.

A knock at her window startled her. She jerked upright, her heart skipping a beat as she turned to see Max's face grinning through the glass, his breath fogging up the pane.

"Max?" she muttered under her breath, crossing the room to unlatch the window. It slid open with a soft creak, and Max wasted no time in climbing through, landing clumsily on her carpet.

"Hey there, sunshine," he said, brushing invisible dust off his jeans. "Hope I'm not interrupting your brooding session."

"Max!" Ella hissed, glancing toward the door. "You could've just knocked on the front door like a normal person."

"And miss my grand entrance? No way."

Before Ella could respond, another knock sounded—this time on her bedroom door. "Ella?" Jada's voice called through. "Are you decent, or is Max already making himself at home?"

Ella sighed and rolled her eyes. "Come in."

Jada stepped inside, holding two steaming mugs in her hands. "You didn't think we were just going to let you sit here and sulk all night, did you?" She offered Ella one of the mugs, the scent of hot cocoa wafting up, rich and sweet.

Ella took it hesitantly, glancing between them. "You didn't have to come over. I'm fine."

Max snorted, collapsing onto her bed with a dramatic groan. "You are *not* fine. You've got that look—you know, the 'everything's hopeless and the world is ending' look."

Jada shot him a glare as she perched neatly on the edge of Ella's desk chair. "What he means is, you don't have to do this alone, Ella."

Ella stared into the swirling cocoa, her fingers warming against the ceramic mug. "It doesn't matter," she muttered. "We showed the mayor everything, and he still doesn't care. What if… what if no one else does either?"

Max sat up, propping his elbows on his knees. "So what? One cranky guy in a suit says no, and you're ready to pack it in? That doesn't sound like the Ella I know."

Jada nodded, her voice calm but firm. "He's wrong, Ella. You know he is. Everything we've found—the letters, the books, the stories—*they matter.* The mayor doesn't get to decide what the library means to people."

Ella looked up at them, her voice small. "But what if it's not enough? What if we try everything, and it doesn't work?"

Max leaned forward, pointing a finger at her. "Then at least we'll know we gave it everything we had. And besides, you think Mrs. Blythe gave up when things got hard? If she could dream big, then so can we."

Jada smiled, her eyes softening. "He's right. The library survived because Mrs. Blythe believed in it. You're doing the same thing. You're picking up where she left off."

Ella let out a slow breath, her grip on the mug tightening. "But what if I fail?"

Max shrugged, his grin softening into something more genuine. "Then we fail *together*. But we're not going to fail, because you're Ella Carter—professional map-reader, clue-finder, and saver of libraries. And we're your team."

Jada smirked. "Even if Max is more of a liability than an asset sometimes."

"Hey!" Max protested, but it only made Ella crack a small smile.

The warmth of their words began to settle over her like a blanket, pushing back the creeping doubt. She looked down at the journal again, her fingers brushing Mrs. Blythe's words. If Mrs. Blythe had believed in the library's soul enough to hide these secrets, then Ella could believe in them too.

"You're right," she said softly, looking up at her friends. "We're not done yet."

"That's the spirit!" Max shot to his feet, pumping a fist into the air. "Team Library never quits!"

Jada rolled her eyes, but her smile was warm. "We'll figure this out, Ella. One step at a time."

Ella looked between them, her chest swelling with gratitude. They had come to remind her of something she'd nearly forgotten: she wasn't alone.

As the three of them sat together, their quiet chatter filling the room, Ella felt a spark of hope reignite. The fight wasn't over—not by a long shot. And no matter what came next, she knew they'd face it together.

Chapter 7
Behind the Mayor's Curtain

The evening air outside the town hall was cool, carrying a faint breeze that rustled the leaves of the trees lining the quiet street. Ella crouched behind a row of hedges near the side of the building, her breath steady and her heart pounding in her chest. She hadn't meant to linger after the council meeting, but something about Mayor Grayson's hurried exit had caught her attention. Now, she was certain she'd made the right decision.

From her hidden vantage point, she could see Grayson pacing under the glow of a streetlamp, his phone pressed to his ear. His usual composed demeanor was gone, replaced by sharp movements and an air of frustration. Ella strained her ears, holding her breath to catch the words carried on the wind.

"I told you, we're on schedule," Grayson snapped, his voice low but urgent. "The vote is just a formality. The council is already onboard. Three weeks, and the library will be out of our way."

Ella's stomach twisted. Her mind raced as she pieced together what he was saying. Out of our way? The words felt like a slap, each syllable dripping with contempt for the place she loved.

There was a pause as Grayson listened to the voice on the other end of the call. His pacing slowed, his tone softening, though his words were no less cutting. "Yes, I understand the value of the land. That's why we're moving quickly. Once the library is gone, the developers can break ground immediately."

Ella's chest tightened as realization dawned. It wasn't just about the library's upkeep costs or its declining usage. The mayor wanted the land. Or rather, someone else wanted it—and Grayson was ready to hand it over.

"Do you have any idea what kind of backlash this could cause if people find out the truth?" the voice on the phone demanded, its volume loud enough for Ella to catch snippets of the conversation.

Grayson stopped pacing, planting his feet firmly as he replied. "No one's going to find out. The library's supporters are too few, and the rest of the town doesn't care. By the time anyone realizes what's happened, it'll be too late."

Ella felt a surge of anger rise in her chest. Her fingers clenched the edge of the hedge as she leaned in closer, desperate to catch every word. Grayson's arrogance, his utter disregard for the people who cherished the library, made her blood boil.

"What about that girl?" the voice on the phone asked suddenly, and Ella froze. "The one who spoke up at the meeting. She seemed pretty determined."

Grayson waved a dismissive hand, even though the person on the other end couldn't see it. "Ella Carter? She's a kid. Let her play her games. By the time she realizes she's out of her depth, the deal will already be done."

Ella bit down on her lip, her fists tightening. Grayson's words stung, but they also fueled her determination. If he thought she was just a kid playing games, he was about to learn how wrong he was.

"What about the legalities?" the voice pressed. "If there's anything buried in that library's history that complicates this sale, it could blow up in our faces."

Grayson's lips pressed into a thin line, his tone dropping to a near whisper that Ella struggled to hear. "There won't be. I've already ensured that any... obstacles are taken care of. Trust me, the council won't go digging."

Ella's thoughts raced. Obstacles? What kind of obstacles was he referring to? She had no doubt he was talking about something—or someone—he'd pushed aside to make this deal happen.

Grayson ended the call abruptly, tucking his phone into his pocket and glancing around. Ella ducked lower behind the hedge, her heart hammering as he turned in her direction. She held her breath, staying perfectly still until he finally sighed and walked away, disappearing into the shadows beyond the streetlamp.

Once she was certain he was gone, Ella let out a shaky breath and crept out from her hiding spot. Her mind buzzed with everything she'd just heard. The stakes were so much higher than she'd realized. This wasn't just about saving the library—

it was about exposing a deliberate plan to erase it for financial gain.

She replayed Grayson's words in her mind: *"Once the library is gone, the developers can break ground immediately."* The land was valuable, and Grayson was willing to sacrifice the library—and the town's history—for his own benefit.

Ella's hands trembled as she pulled out her phone and dialed quickly. The call connected after two rings.

"Ella?" Jada's voice was groggy, clearly pulled from sleep. "What's going on?"

"I found something," Ella said, her voice shaking with urgency. "Or rather, I heard something. It's bad, Jada. Really bad."

"What are you talking about?" Jada asked, her tone sharpening with concern.

"It's Grayson," Ella said. "He's selling out the library for the land. It's all about money and developers, and he doesn't care who gets hurt in the process. He's hiding something—maybe a lot of things."

There was a pause on the other end before Jada replied, her voice resolute. "We need to meet. Tomorrow. First thing."

"Agreed," Ella said. "I'll tell the others. But Jada, this changes everything. We're not just fighting to save the library anymore. We're fighting to stop whatever Grayson's planning."

"Then we'd better make sure we're ready," Jada said. "Because it sounds like he's not playing fair."

Ella ended the call and slipped her phone back into her pocket. The cool night air did little to calm her racing heart. The library wasn't just a building anymore—it was the center of a battle for the soul of Blythewood, and she wasn't going to let Grayson win. Not without a fight.

The library was quiet as the morning sunlight streamed through its high windows, casting long, golden beams across the dusty floor. Ella sat at the edge of the librarian's desk, her knee bouncing with nervous energy. The events of the night before weighed heavily on her mind. Mayor Grayson's words kept replaying, each one sharper than the last. She glanced toward Mrs. Pearlson, who was meticulously organizing a stack of returned books, her movements calm but deliberate.

"Mrs. Pearlson," Ella began hesitantly, breaking the silence. "Can I ask you something?"

The librarian looked up, her sharp eyes softening as they met Ella's. "Of course, dear. What's on your mind?"

Ella hesitated, then plunged ahead. "What do you know about Mrs. Blythe? I mean, really know about her. Not just the usual stuff about her founding the library."

Mrs. Pearlson paused, her fingers lingering on the edge of a book. She studied Ella for a moment before speaking. "Why do you ask?"

Ella shifted, her voice lowering. "I overheard something last night. Mayor Grayson—he's planning to sell the library's land to developers. And it's not just about money; there's something bigger going on. I think it's connected to the library's history, to the things Mrs. Blythe left behind."

Mrs. Pearlson's expression tightened, a flicker of worry crossing her face. She set the book down carefully and gestured for Ella to sit. "That's a serious accusation, Ella. You're certain about what you heard?"

"I'm certain," Ella said firmly. "And if we're going to stop him, I need to understand why this library matters so much. Not just to me, but to the town."

Mrs. Pearlson exhaled slowly, her gaze drifting toward the shelves that lined the library. "Evelyn Blythe was more than just a librarian," she began, her voice quiet but steady. "She was a visionary. She believed that stories had the power to shape people, to build communities, and to preserve history. When she founded this library, she didn't just want it to be a place where people borrowed books. She wanted it to be the heart of Blythewood."

Ella leaned forward, her interest piqued. "The heart of Blythewood? What does that mean?"

Mrs. Pearlson smiled faintly, her eyes distant as if she were recalling a memory. "To Evelyn, the library wasn't just a building. She called it a living thing. She believed every book on its shelves carried a piece of the person who had read it, that their thoughts, dreams, and experiences lingered here. She used to say that if you listened closely, you could hear the library breathing."

"That's beautiful," Ella murmured. "But how does that connect to what Grayson's doing?"

Mrs. Pearlson's expression darkened. "When Evelyn passed, she left behind more than just the books. She left behind a legacy—a collection of items that represented the town's history. She called them the 'soul of the library.' I've always believed she hid them somewhere within these walls, though I've never been able to find them."

Ella's breath caught. "You think the vault we found could be part of that?"

Mrs. Pearlson nodded slowly. "It's possible. Evelyn was meticulous, and she would have ensured that those items were protected. If the vault contains what I suspect it does, it's more than just a collection. It's proof of the library's importance to Blythewood."

Ella's mind raced. The books in the vault, each with its own story and dedication, were more than just relics—they were tangible evidence of the library's role in preserving the town's identity. But the thought of Grayson's plans made her stomach churn.

"What do we do?" Ella asked, her voice trembling with urgency. "How do we make people see how much this library means before it's too late?"

Mrs. Pearlson reached across the desk, her hand resting gently on Ella's. "We tell the story, Ella. Not just Evelyn's story, but the story of everyone who has ever walked through these doors. The people who left their mark on this library and the people whose lives it has touched. That's how we show them its worth."

Ella swallowed hard, her resolve strengthening. "And the vault? If we reveal it, won't that just make it a target? What if the developers try to take everything and move it somewhere else?"

Mrs. Pearlson's eyes narrowed, her determination mirroring Ella's. "That's why we must act carefully. We need to rally the community, show them what's at stake. Once they understand what this library holds—its history, its soul—they won't let it go without a fight."

Ella nodded, her mind already buzzing with ideas. "We can organize an event, something that brings people together. We'll share the stories, the dedications in the books. We'll make them see that this isn't just about saving a building—it's about saving who we are."

Mrs. Pearlson smiled, a glimmer of hope lighting her tired eyes. "Evelyn would be proud of you, Ella. She always believed that the right person would come along to protect this place when it needed it most. I think that person is you."

Ella felt a lump form in her throat, but she pushed it down, her determination burning brighter. "I won't let Grayson win," she said firmly. "Not while I'm still standing."

Mrs. Pearlson squeezed her hand gently before releasing it. "Then let's get to work. We have a story to tell, and not much time to tell it."

As Ella rose to her feet, she glanced around the library with fresh eyes. It wasn't just a sanctuary or a refuge anymore—it was a battleground. And she was ready to fight for it with everything she had.

The group sat in a tight circle on the floor of Ella's living room, the faint hum of a floor lamp the only sound filling the silence that had stretched uncomfortably for several minutes. The gold bookmark lay in the center of the circle like an artifact in a museum, catching the light with its delicate engraving: *Every story leads to another.*" Around it were scattered photographs Jada had taken of the vault, pages of notes Ella had scrawled, and a tablet displaying a digital version of the map.

"Okay," Ella began, breaking the silence. She leaned forward, her elbows on her knees. "We have something amazing. The vault proves that the library is more than just a building. It's a piece of this town's history. Now we need to figure out how to make everyone else see that."

"Easier said than done," Noah replied, leaning back against the couch. His arms were crossed, and his expression was skeptical. "You think showing people some old books is going to stop the council from selling the library to developers?"

Max threw a hand up in mock frustration. "Oh, great. Here comes Noah, the voice of doom and gloom. Do you have to shoot down every plan before we've even started?"

"I'm not shooting it down," Noah said evenly, though his tone sharpened. "I'm being realistic. The council doesn't care about books, Max. They care about money. They care about numbers."

"And that's exactly why we need to show them the numbers that matter," Jada interjected, swiping through photos on her tablet. "Look at these inscriptions. Each one represents a person who cared enough about this library to leave a piece of themselves behind. If we can show that to the community, we can create enough noise that the council won't be able to ignore us."

Noah sighed, shaking his head. "You're assuming the community will care. Most people haven't set foot in the library in years."

Ella's jaw tightened. "Maybe that's because no one's reminded them why they should care. We have to make them see that this isn't just about a building. It's about their stories, their families, their memories."

Max leaned forward, a grin spreading across his face. "Exactly! We make it personal. Hit them in the feels. That's my specialty."

"Your specialty is making everything about you," Jada muttered, not looking up from her screen.

"Exactly," Max said with a wink. "And if I can convince people I'm worth paying attention to, we can definitely convince them the library is."

Ella let out a soft laugh despite the tension, but Noah's expression remained serious. "And what happens when Grayson and the developers find out about the vault?" he asked, his voice steady but challenging. "Do you really think they're just going to let us parade it around without trying to take control?"

"That's why we have to be strategic," Jada said, her tone firm. "We don't reveal the vault right away. We use the dedications and the history to build interest first. Get people talking, get the community on our side. Once we have their support, we can present the vault as the centerpiece of our argument."

"And what if it backfires?" Noah pressed. "What if we lose control of the narrative and the council spins it against us? They could argue the vault would be safer in a museum or private collection."

Ella clenched her fists, frustration bubbling to the surface. "So what are you saying, Noah? That we do nothing? That we just sit back and let Grayson sell off the library like it's a piece of scrap land?"

"No," Noah said firmly, meeting her gaze. "I'm saying we need to think this through. If we rush into this without considering the risks, we could lose everything. I'm not trying to stop you, Ella—I'm trying to make sure we don't screw this up."

The room fell silent again, the weight of Noah's words settling over them. Ella exhaled slowly, her anger giving way to understanding. He wasn't trying to undermine them; he was trying to protect them.

"You're right," she said finally, her voice quiet but steady. "We can't afford to make mistakes. But we also can't afford to wait too long. Grayson isn't going to give us time to figure this out."

"So what's the plan, then?" Max asked, glancing around the circle. "How do we do this without blowing it?"

Ella leaned forward, her determination reigniting. "We start small. We focus on the dedications first—share the stories behind them. Jada, you can use the photos and create a presentation. Something we can show at a community meeting or an event."

Jada nodded, her fingers already tapping on her tablet. "I can make a digital timeline of the library's history, highlighting the dedications and their significance."

"Noah," Ella continued, turning to him, "you're good at logistics. Help me figure out how to present this in a way that feels grounded, like something the council can't dismiss."

Noah hesitated for a moment before nodding. "Fine. But we need contingency plans in case something goes wrong."

"And me?" Max asked, his tone lighter but his expression serious. "What's my role in this epic quest?"

Ella smirked. "You're the face of the operation. You're going to help us rally the community—get people to show up, care, and speak out."

Max's grin widened. "I knew I was born for greatness."

Despite the tension, the group shared a small laugh. The stakes were higher than ever, but in that moment, they felt a renewed sense of purpose. Together, they could fight for the library. Together, they could protect its legacy.

"Alright," Ella said, standing and looking around at her friends. "We have a lot of work to do, and not much time to do it. Let's get started."

As they began gathering their materials, Ella felt a flicker of hope. The road ahead wouldn't be easy, but they had a plan—and more importantly, they had each other.

Chapter 8
The Soul of the Library

The library's reading room was a hive of energy, alive with the hushed voices of Ella, Max, Jada, and Noah as they huddled around one of the long tables. Papers, sketches, and hastily scribbled notes were spread out across its surface like puzzle pieces waiting to come together.

Max, sitting backward on a chair, pointed at the stack of ideas they'd already written down. "Alright, people. We've got one shot at this. *Blythewood Library Day*—the event to end all events. What do we want, and how do we make it awesome?"

Jada pushed her glasses up and tapped her stylus against her tablet. "We need more than awesome. We need impactful. If this is going to work, it has to make people feel something. Make them *see* what the library means."

"Agreed," Noah said, leaning forward, his arms crossed as he studied their notes. "So, where do we start? What's the hook?"

Ella looked up from the blueprint she'd been sketching over, her voice steady but hopeful. "The stories. We start with the stories. The letters, the bookmarks, and Mrs. Blythe's plans—those will be the heart of the event."

Max nodded enthusiastically, spinning his chair around. "Okay, I'm seeing it—an exhibit. Big displays, tables full of the letters, the dedications, photos of the old books. Like a time capsule exploded, but, you know, in a cool way."

Jada smirked. "A 'cool explosion'? That's… not quite how I'd put it, but the idea works. We'll create stations where people can walk through and see everything for themselves—photos, artifacts, even recordings of the letters being read aloud."

Noah raised an eyebrow. "Recordings?"

Jada shrugged, already jotting notes onto her tablet. "Why not? We can get people from the community to read them. Imagine walking into the exhibit and hearing Mrs. Blythe's impact in their own voices. It'll make the stories feel alive again."

"I love that," Ella said, her face lighting up. "It's personal. It connects the past to the present."

"Exactly." Jada shot her a small smile before returning to her notes.

"Okay, what else?" Max jumped in, his energy palpable. "This isn't just a history thing—we need some pizzazz, something that makes people *want* to show up. Like, I don't know… performances?"

Noah frowned. "Performances?"

"Yeah, like live readings," Max explained, gesturing wildly. "We get kids, families, maybe even local teachers to read excerpts from the books in the library. You know, the classics—stuff people will recognize."

"That's not a bad idea," Ella said, warming to it. "It would remind people of what's here, what's been waiting for them this whole time."

"Or poetry," Jada suggested, scribbling it down. "People could perform their own poems or short stories about what the library means to them. Like an open mic."

Noah leaned back, considering. "You're talking about a whole program. Exhibits, performances… we'd need a schedule to keep it organized."

"I can do that," Jada said quickly, her eyes already flicking to her tablet. "I'll draw up a rough agenda tonight—slots for readings, performances, and breaks for people to explore the displays."

"And what about food?" Max added, leaning across the table. "You *cannot* have an event without food. It's, like, a universal law."

Ella laughed softly. "We could ask local businesses to help—donate snacks, maybe set up a small stand. If people see the community rallying behind the library, it'll make a bigger impact."

Noah nodded. "I'll talk to my dad. He knows a lot of the shop owners downtown. If they hear what we're doing, some of them might help out."

"Perfect." Ella looked around the table, feeling the momentum building like a wave. "So, we've got exhibits with the letters and blueprints, readings and performances, maybe even food. What about a way to raise money? The mayor's still going to ask how we plan to *fund* this."

Jada's brows furrowed thoughtfully. "We could sell tickets, but that might turn people away."

"Donations," Max said instantly, snapping his fingers. "We make it free to come, but we'll set up jars or a digital option for people to donate. And not just money—maybe books too. A 'rebuild the library' drive."

"That's brilliant," Ella said, smiling. "It's not just about saving what's here. It's about building something better. Mrs. Blythe's plans, our plans—something for the future."

The table fell quiet for a moment, the weight of their task settling over them. Noah broke the silence, his voice steady. "This can work. If we pull it off, if we get the town to see what we've seen, the library has a chance."

"It's more than a chance," Max said, grinning confidently. "It's going to *happen.*"

Jada glanced at Ella. "You ready for this?"

Ella looked down at the blueprint of Mrs. Blythe's dream, the faded ink now surrounded by their scribbled notes and sketches. For the first time, she could see it clearly—the event, the people, the way the library would come alive again.

"I'm ready," she said firmly, meeting their eyes. "We're going to show the town what the library really means. And we're not giving up."

Max shot his fist into the air. "Blythewood Library Day, here we come!"

The room filled with quiet laughter, the tension breaking as they gathered their notes. In the fading light of the library, surrounded by books and memories, Ella felt something she hadn't in a long time—certainty. They had a plan, they had each other, and they had something worth fighting for.

This wasn't just about saving the library anymore. It was about honoring its past and building a future where stories—and the people who loved them—could thrive.

The town square buzzed with the sounds of everyday life— doors creaking open, conversations floating on the breeze, and the occasional car rumbling over cobblestones. Ella stood near a fold-out table stacked with flyers for *Blythewood Library Day*, her heart tight with both hope and trepidation. Max, Jada, and Noah worked nearby, handing out flyers to passersby and talking up the event to anyone who'd stop to listen.

"Thank you so much for your support," Ella said brightly to Mrs. Hayworth, one of the older residents who paused to take a flyer.

"I'll be there, dear," Mrs. Hayworth replied with a kind smile, tucking the paper into her bag. "The library means a great deal to me. My children practically grew up there."

Ella's smile widened, relief flooding through her. "That's exactly why we're doing this. We hope to see you there."

Mrs. Hayworth patted her arm gently before walking away, and for a brief moment, Ella felt like they were gaining momentum. But then another voice cut through the calm.

"Library Day, huh?"

Ella turned to see Mr. Callum, a local shop owner, standing a few feet away with his arms crossed. His sharp gaze flicked to the stack of flyers on the table. "What's this supposed to do? Convince us all to save that dusty old building?"

"We're not just saving a building," Ella replied carefully, trying to keep her voice steady. "We're saving what it means to the community."

Callum snorted, shaking his head. "Sentimental nonsense. You're wasting your time, kid. That land could be put to real use—something that actually helps the town."

"It does help the town," Noah said, stepping up beside Ella. His voice was calm, but there was a weight to it. "The library has always been more than just a building. It's history. It's a place where people find belonging."

Callum frowned, his tone dismissive. "Belonging won't fix the economy. You kids don't understand how the real world works. It's time to move on."

Ella opened her mouth to respond, but Callum was already turning away, muttering under his breath.

"Let him go," Noah said quietly, placing a hand on her shoulder. "Some people won't listen, no matter what we say."

Ella nodded, but the sting of his words lingered. Across the square, she spotted Jada talking to a small group of teenagers. Two of them eagerly took flyers, but the third shook his head, laughing loudly.

"What's the point?" he said, his voice carrying across the square. "It's just a bunch of old books. Nobody even goes to the library anymore."

Jada's lips tightened, but she didn't back down. "It's more than that. You might not need it, but other people do. It's about the community."

"Sure," the teen scoffed, rolling his eyes. "Good luck with that." He turned and walked off, leaving Jada standing there, visibly frustrated.

Max came bounding up a moment later, his hands full of crumpled flyers. "Okay, so—good news and bad news," he announced, his usual grin slightly dimmed. "Good news: Mrs. McNally offered to bake cookies for the event. Bad news: Mr. Benson laughed in my face and called the library a 'money pit.'"

"Wonderful," Jada muttered as she rejoined the group, her expression tight. "I just got told the library's irrelevant. Twice."

Ella exhaled slowly, trying to keep the doubt creeping into her chest at bay. "Some people don't understand. But there are others who do."

"Yeah," Max said quickly, trying to rally the mood. "Like Mrs. McNally! Cookies are a win, right?"

"It's a start," Noah said, though his tone was measured. "But we're hitting resistance, and it's not going to stop. People want to believe in the library, but they don't think it's practical."

Ella looked out over the square, watching as people passed by their table—some taking flyers with polite nods, others shaking their heads or ignoring them entirely. The energy she'd felt that morning was beginning to waver, replaced by an ache of uncertainty.

"Maybe they're right," she whispered before she could stop herself.

Jada's head snapped toward her. "No, they're not."

"But what if this isn't enough?" Ella pressed, her voice lower now. "What if people just… don't care?"

"They care," Noah said firmly, meeting her gaze. "You've seen it. Not everyone, but enough people to make a difference. We just have to push harder. Show them why it matters."

Jada crossed her arms, her eyes narrowing thoughtfully. "We're not going to win everyone over, Ella. But we don't need to. We just need enough voices to get through to the council."

"Exactly," Max added, stepping beside them. "We've got cookies, flyers, and the best team in town. Don't lose hope now, Captain."

Ella managed a small smile at that, though the knot of doubt in her chest hadn't fully disappeared. She looked down at the stack of flyers on the table, then back out at the square.

"Let's keep going," she said quietly, straightening her shoulders. "We're not done yet."

As they returned to handing out flyers, the reactions remained mixed—smiles, dismissals, promises, and scoffs. But for every "it's not worth it," there was someone like Mrs. Hayworth, clutching the flyer with quiet reverence. And for now, Ella held onto that.

Even if it wasn't easy, even if they faced resistance, they weren't giving up. The library deserved their fight.

The library felt different in the fading light, its towering shelves casting long, narrow shadows across the floor. The group sat slumped around the reading room table, a day's worth of rejection etched across their faces. Ella stared down at the half-empty stack of flyers, her fingers idly tracing the paper's edge.

Max broke the silence with a sigh, tossing a crumpled flyer into the middle of the table. "Well, that was brutal. I didn't think people could be so…" He waved his hands vaguely. "Anti-library."

"It's like some of them *want* to lose it," Jada muttered, her tablet abandoned in front of her as she rubbed her temples. "I don't get it. How can you scoff at saving something so important?"

Noah, arms crossed and brow furrowed, shook his head. "They're scared. Change doesn't come easy for people when they think they're fighting to survive. It doesn't make them right, but… I get it."

Ella looked up, her voice soft. "Maybe we're fighting a losing battle."

The words hung in the air like a weight no one wanted to claim.

"That's nonsense, dear."

All four of them turned toward the voice. Mrs. Pearlson stood in the doorway of the reading room, her cardigan pulled tight around her shoulders, her small frame exuding an unshakable warmth despite the shadows around her. She stepped into the room with slow, deliberate steps, her gaze settling on Ella.

"You're not losing any battle," she said firmly.

Ella's cheeks burned as she glanced away. "It doesn't feel like we're winning either."

Mrs. Pearlson smiled faintly, her eyes crinkling with quiet understanding. "When you're fighting for something that matters, it rarely feels easy. And, believe me, this library *matters*."

She moved closer to the table, placing a hand on the back of one of the chairs. Her voice softened, but it carried the weight of someone who had spent a lifetime holding spaces like these together. "Do you know why I stayed here all these years? Why I've kept this place running even when no one else cared to notice?"

Jada sat up straighter, curiosity flickering in her eyes. "Why?"

"Because this library saved me," Mrs. Pearlson said simply. She looked around the room, her voice growing stronger. "When I was young—oh, I must've been no older than you, Ella—I spent most of my days here. I'd sit in the back corner with my nose buried in a book because it was the only place I felt safe. The only place that felt like home."

Ella blinked, surprised. "I… I didn't know that."

Mrs. Pearlson smiled again, the kind of smile that carried memories. "And I'm not the only one. For every person who scoffs, there's someone who found their refuge here, just like I did. Just like you and your friends have. Don't let a few doubters shake your belief."

Max sat up suddenly, his voice lighter but sincere. "Yeah! I mean, you should've seen Mrs. McNally earlier—she was ready to bake the entire library cookies to keep it open. People *do* care. We just need to remind them how much."

Mrs. Pearlson nodded approvingly. "And you'll do just that. I've seen the flyers, and I've heard about your event. It's ambitious, but it's exactly what we need. Sometimes people need to see a dream before they believe in it."

"But what if it's not enough?" Ella asked quietly, her voice barely above a whisper.

Mrs. Pearlson moved to stand beside her, placing a hand gently on her shoulder. "Ella, what you're doing is more than enough. You're giving this library a voice again. You're standing up for something that most people would've let fade away. That's no small thing."

Noah, who had been quiet for a while, leaned forward, his tone steady. "She's right. This isn't just about convincing the council anymore. It's about showing the town what's been here all along."

"Exactly," Jada added, a spark of determination returning to her voice. "We'll organize the event, make it perfect—exhibits, performances, the whole thing. If people see what the library means to the community, they'll rally around it."

Max grinned, thumping the table lightly with his fist. "And we'll make it fun. People can't resist a good story—and we've got plenty to share."

Ella looked around at her friends, their faces alive again with determination. Mrs. Pearlson's words settled over her like a balm, quieting the doubts that had gnawed at her all day. Slowly, she sat up straighter, a small smile tugging at her lips.

"Then let's do it," she said firmly. "We'll make Blythewood Library Day something no one can ignore."

"That's the spirit," Mrs. Pearlson said warmly. "And you won't be doing it alone. I'll help however I can. I may not move as fast as I used to, but I still know a thing or two about organizing events."

Max shot Mrs. Pearlson a cheeky grin. "I knew we could count on you."

Jada smirked, jotting notes back onto her tablet. "Between the four of us and Mrs. Pearlson, we've got this covered."

Ella exhaled, her chest feeling lighter than it had all day. She glanced toward Mrs. Pearlson, who looked at her with a mix of pride and quiet faith.

"Thank you," Ella said softly. "For believing in us."

Mrs. Pearlson gave her shoulder a gentle squeeze. "You don't need my belief, dear. You just need to trust in your own."

The group shared a look—a moment of unspoken unity—before turning back to the table. Plans began to flow again, ideas bouncing from one person to the next as energy hummed through the room. Ella felt it too: the rallying cry that started small but now carried the weight of something far bigger.

Together, they would show the town what the library meant—and what it could still become.

Chapter 9
A Plan Takes Shape

The Blythewood Town Hall buzzed with low murmurs and shuffling feet, the kind of energy that built just before a storm. Residents packed the small room, some standing against the back wall, others perched on the edges of their seats. The tension in the air was thick, crackling like a live wire. Ella stood near the center with Max, Jada, and Noah clustered around her, all four of them watching as Mayor Grayson approached the podium.

Mayor Grayson cleared his throat, the microphone amplifying the small sound into something sharper. He adjusted his tie, his usual calm demeanor masking the unease behind his eyes.

"Thank you for coming on such short notice," he began, his voice carrying through the room. "I understand there have been strong feelings surrounding the fate of the Blythewood Library, and as mayor, it's my responsibility to keep this town's best interests in mind."

Max leaned toward Ella, muttering under his breath, "I don't like where this is going."

"Me neither," Ella whispered back, clutching her notebook tightly.

The mayor's gaze swept over the crowd, lingering briefly on Ella's group before he continued. "The developers interested in the library's land have increased their offer. Doubled it, in fact."

The room erupted in gasps and low, murmured conversations. People twisted in their chairs to whisper to their neighbors, eyebrows raised in disbelief.

"Doubled?" Jada hissed, her voice tight. "That's impossible."

"It's not impossible," Noah said quietly, his jaw clenched. "They're trying to lock this in before the town can think twice."

Ella's heart sank as the mayor raised his hand for silence.

"I know this is difficult to hear," Mayor Grayson said, his tone polished and deliberate. "But this offer represents a real opportunity for Blythewood. With this funding, we can invest in new infrastructure, revitalize businesses, and secure the economic future of our town."

An older man near the front stood up, his voice shaking. "What about the library, Mayor? What about everything it's done for this town?"

Grayson's expression remained calm, though his voice softened slightly. "I appreciate the sentiment, Mr. Clarkson, truly. But sentiment does not keep our economy running. The library, while historic, has become unsustainable. This bid is a lifeline for us all."

Ella felt Max shift beside her, his energy vibrating like a live wire. "He's selling them on numbers," he muttered. "No one's even thinking about what we found."

"Not yet," Jada replied through gritted teeth.

Another voice rang out from the back of the room—a woman Ella recognized as the owner of the diner downtown. "And what happens to the library, Mayor? That building's been here longer than most of us!"

The mayor spread his hands, his voice measured. "I understand the emotional weight of this decision. But we cannot cling to the past at the expense of the future. We need jobs. We need growth."

Max couldn't take it anymore. He shot to his feet. "That's not fair!"

Heads turned toward him, and Ella's stomach twisted as she grabbed his arm. "Max—"

"No, Ella," Max said firmly, his voice rising. "We've been working day and night to show everyone what the library really means. We found letters, blueprints—plans Mrs. Blythe left behind for this town. She believed in the library's future, and we should too."

The room fell silent for a beat. Mayor Grayson's gaze locked onto Max, and though he smiled faintly, there was a flicker of annoyance in his eyes.

"Young man," Grayson said, his voice smooth but firm, "I respect your passion, but the reality of the situation cannot be ignored. This offer is concrete, and it will benefit everyone."

Ella stood then, her voice steady despite the way her hands shook. "You're wrong, Mayor Grayson."

The mayor's eyebrows lifted slightly, but Ella pressed on, her words ringing through the room. "The library isn't a drain—it's part of who we are. We've spent weeks gathering proof that it's more than just a building. It's history, it's community, and it's people. If you tear it down, you're tearing down the heart of this town."

A murmur rippled through the crowd. Some faces turned toward her with curiosity; others looked skeptical, their brows furrowed in doubt.

Grayson's smile remained fixed. "And while I admire your efforts, Miss Carter, sentiment alone will not build new roads or save struggling businesses."

Jada shot up next, tablet clutched tightly in her hands. "You're talking about destroying something irreplaceable for money that might not even solve the town's real problems. People don't need a shopping center—they need places where they can feel safe, where they can learn and connect."

More murmurs, louder this time.

Noah stood, his quiet presence cutting through the rising tension. "If the developers cared about Blythewood, they wouldn't be trying so hard to take something this important away. You don't need to destroy the library to save the town."

Mayor Grayson raised a hand again, his voice louder now. "Please, everyone. I understand this is an emotional topic. A vote will be held soon, and the council will decide based on what is best for Blythewood as a whole."

Ella looked out at the crowd, searching for faces that mirrored the belief she felt deep in her chest. Some people avoided her gaze, shifting nervously in their seats, but others—like Mrs. Hayworth and Mrs. Pearlson, who stood near the back— nodded quietly.

As Mayor Grayson stepped back from the podium, Ella sank back into her seat. The murmurs swirled around her, a mix of doubt and hope.

Max leaned closer, his voice low. "We're not giving up, El. We'll make them see."

Ella nodded, though the weight of the mayor's words hung heavy over her. "We have to. Before it's too late."

Noah glanced toward the podium, his expression firm. "We've still got time. And we're not backing down."

As the meeting continued, the tension remained, unresolved but alive. The developers' threat loomed large, but Ella refused to let it drown out their fight. She gripped her notebook, Mrs. Blythe's plans echoing in her mind.

The library's future wasn't decided yet—and they weren't done fighting for it.

The community center was packed, the kind of crowd that hummed with pent-up tension. Rows of chairs filled the room, with latecomers forced to stand along the walls or hover near the back. The air was thick with the hum of overlapping conversations, voices rising and falling like the tide.

Ella stood near the front with Max, Jada, and Noah by her side. She clutched the library's journal in her hands, her palms damp as she ran through what she wanted to say. From where she stood, she could already see familiar faces—Mrs. Pearlson, Mrs. Hayworth, and a few others who supported their cause—but there were plenty more whose expressions ranged from skeptical to outright hostile.

Mayor Grayson was seated at the center of the stage, his expression carefully neutral as he prepared to moderate the meeting. Beside him sat two members of the town council, their notepads open, pens poised as though the outcome of the evening depended on what they wrote.

"Let's begin," Grayson said, his voice amplified by the microphone. "I want to remind everyone to keep this discussion civil. Emotions are running high, but we're here to find the best path forward for Blythewood."

A middle-aged man stood up near the front. Ella recognized him—Mr. Callum, the shop owner who had dismissed them in the square. He cleared his throat, his voice sharp. "Let's stop dancing around the issue. The developers' offer is a gift. Doubling the bid gives this town a real chance—something it hasn't had in years."

Several murmurs of agreement rippled through the room.

"But at what cost?" Mrs. Hayworth's voice broke through as she stood up, her small frame unshakable. "You're talking about selling the heart of this town. A place that's given generations a place to learn, to dream, to feel safe. You can't just replace that with a strip mall."

Callum scoffed, throwing a dismissive hand in the air. "Safe? Come on, Mrs. Hayworth. No one uses that library anymore. It's falling apart. How much longer are we supposed to pour money into a building that doesn't earn anything back?"

"Because it's not just a building!"

Ella hadn't realized she was the one who'd spoken until the room turned toward her. Her voice shook as she stepped forward, clutching the journal against her chest.

"It's not just bricks and shelves," she said, forcing herself to continue. "The library *means* something. It's history, it's stories, it's a place that's given people a reason to believe in themselves when they had nowhere else to go."

A few nods came from the back, but someone near the middle shook their head. "It's easy for you kids to talk about stories, but stories don't pay bills," a man called out, earning a few murmurs of approval.

Ella's heart thudded, but she pushed on. "Then what about the stories of people who came here to find hope? We found letters—dozens of them—thanking the library for helping them through hard times. It's been more than a building to so many people."

"And we found *plans,*" Jada added, standing up beside her. "Blueprints Mrs. Blythe left behind. She had a vision for this library's future—an expanded reading room, gardens, and spaces for the community. She believed the library could grow with the town."

Mayor Grayson raised a hand to quiet the room. "Let's stay focused, please. Does anyone else wish to speak?"

A tall woman in the back stood up, her arms crossed over her chest. "And where's the money for all of that going to come from? Who's paying for this vision you're talking about? Because it sure isn't the council."

Her words drew a smattering of applause, and Ella's stomach twisted as she watched heads nodding around the room. The room was starting to divide, like cracks splitting through the center.

Max jumped in, unable to stay quiet. "Look, we get it! Money matters, okay? But what happens when you sell the library? You get cash now, sure, but you lose something that can never come back. How does that help anyone?"

"It's not enough!" a man shouted back. "The town needs jobs, not memories!"

Voices erupted all at once—people arguing from every corner of the room, their words colliding like thunderclaps. Some defended the library, others demanded progress, and the shouting rose to a cacophony that made Ella's head spin.

"Quiet, please!" Grayson called, but the noise rolled on, impossible to contain.

Ella turned to Jada and Noah, her voice low. "They're not listening."

"They will," Noah said, though his voice wasn't entirely steady. "We just have to keep trying."

"Are you sure?" Jada muttered, glancing around at the swirling arguments. "It feels like we're losing them."

Ella swallowed hard, forcing herself to breathe. Finally, she stepped forward, raising her voice as best she could. "Please! Just listen!"

The room quieted enough for her voice to carry, but the crowd's energy remained volatile, their eyes on her. She took a shaky breath, her voice softer now but clear.

"We're not asking you to pick history over the future. We're asking you to see how the two can work together. Mrs. Blythe believed in this library because she knew it could *grow*. So do we. We're offering you more than a short-term solution. We're offering a way to build something that lasts."

The room fell into an uneasy silence. For a moment, Ella thought she'd broken through—but then someone scoffed, loud enough to cut through the stillness. "That's a nice speech, kid, but it doesn't change reality."

Mayor Grayson rose then, his voice calm but firm. "Thank you, Miss Carter. We appreciate your passion. The council will continue to discuss all options. For now, this meeting is adjourned."

The gavel came down with a sharp *crack,* and the room erupted into chatter again. Ella's shoulders slumped as she stepped back, her confidence unraveling.

"They didn't listen," she whispered, her voice barely audible.

Max clapped a hand on her shoulder. "Not yet. But they will."

Jada nodded, her jaw tight with determination. "This isn't over, Ella. Not even close."

Noah looked toward the leaving crowd, his expression unreadable. "We just have to work harder. They're divided now, but we can still get through to them."

As the room emptied, Ella held onto their words, even as doubt gnawed at her resolve. The fight to save the library wasn't over, but tonight had proven one thing: it was going to be harder than she ever imagined.

The heavy thud of the mayor's gavel echoed through the now-empty town hall like a final, ominous note. Rows of chairs sat abandoned, the faint hum of fluorescent lights buzzing overhead. Ella stood in the quiet, her hands still gripping the edges of her notebook, her knuckles pale against the worn cover. The meeting had ended, but the weight of it lingered in the air, pressing down on her chest.

Max kicked at one of the empty chairs with the toe of his shoe, his voice breaking the silence. "That… did not go well."

Jada shot him a sharp look as she stood near the table, organizing her scattered notes. "Understatement of the year, Max."

"I'm just saying what we're all thinking!" Max huffed, running a hand through his hair. "Half the room was ready to bulldoze the library *tonight*."

Noah, who had been standing quietly by the window, finally turned to face them. "We're not done yet. They didn't shut us down completely."

Before Ella could respond, the sound of approaching footsteps made them all stiffen. Mayor Grayson stepped back into the room, his polished shoes clicking against the tile as he moved toward them. His expression was calm, unreadable as always, but his gaze was sharp when it settled on Ella.

"Miss Carter," he began, stopping a few feet away. "I wanted a word."

Ella straightened, her throat tight as she nodded. "Yes, sir?"

Grayson clasped his hands behind his back, his tone measured. "It's clear that you and your friends are… determined. I can't deny that."

"Because we care," Jada said quickly, stepping forward.

The mayor's lips twitched faintly at the corner, though it wasn't quite a smile. "Caring is admirable, but it isn't enough to change the numbers. The developers have made an offer the council can't ignore. However…" He paused, letting the word hang in the air for a beat. "I believe in giving everyone a fair chance."

Ella's heart skipped, a flicker of hope lighting up her chest. "What do you mean?"

"You have one month," Grayson said simply, his gaze unwavering. "If you can raise enough funds to counter the developers' bid—or at least prove you have serious financial backing—then we'll reconsider. But if you fail to meet that deadline, the council will move forward with the sale."

"One month?" Max repeated, his voice tinged with disbelief. "That's barely any time!"

"Time isn't on our side," Grayson replied curtly. "The developers won't wait forever, and neither can we."

Jada looked up from her tablet, her voice sharp. "And how are we supposed to raise that much money in a month? We're just a group of kids."

The mayor's expression didn't change. "That's not my concern. You wanted a chance, and now you have it." He glanced toward Ella again, his voice softening just slightly. "Prove that the library matters, Miss Carter. Not just in sentiment, but in value."

Ella swallowed hard, her mind already spinning. "We will."

Grayson gave a small nod, then turned and walked back toward the door, leaving the echo of his footsteps behind him. When the door clicked shut, the room fell into an uneasy silence.

Max flopped into a chair with a groan, throwing his hands up. "A month! Does he think we have a magic money tree?"

"We don't need magic," Noah said quietly, though his brow was furrowed in thought. "We need a plan. And fast."

Jada sighed, pinching the bridge of her nose. "He's testing us. He thinks we'll give up."

Ella shook her head, her voice steady despite the chaos swirling in her mind. "We won't."

Max looked up at her, skeptical. "El, this is huge. We're talking thousands of dollars. I mean, how do we even start?"

Ella stared at the empty stage where the mayor had stood moments earlier, the flicker of hope in her chest hardening into something sharper—determination. "We do what we've been doing. We rally the town. We show them the blueprints, the letters, the plans. If we can make them believe in the library again, we'll find a way."

Jada's gaze sharpened as she turned to face Ella fully. "You're serious?"

"I have to be," Ella replied. "We *all* have to be. This is it. This is our chance to save the library."

Noah nodded, stepping closer to the table. "Then let's start breaking this down. We need a fundraiser—something big enough to get the town's attention and get people invested."

"Blythewood Library Day is already a start," Jada said, quickly pulling up the plans on her tablet. "If we turn it into a fundraiser too—donations, auctions, even small ticket sales—it might work."

Max sat up straighter, a grin tugging at his lips. "And we can pull in local businesses! Mrs. McNally's already on board with cookies—imagine what we could do with more support."

Ella's chest swelled with a mix of fear and determination as she looked at her friends. "It's not going to be easy," she said softly. "But we don't have a choice. We either make this work, or we lose everything."

Jada nodded firmly. "Then we make it work."

"We go big," Max added, his grin widening. "Bigger than the mayor's wildest expectations."

Noah gave a small, steady nod. "One step at a time. We'll figure this out."

Ella tightened her grip on the notebook, feeling the weight of Mrs. Blythe's vision pressing against her palms. One month. One chance. It wasn't much, but it was enough to fight for.

"Then let's get to work," she said.

They moved as one, gathering their notes and sketches, already throwing ideas into the air as they made their way out of the empty town hall. The shadows outside stretched long under the evening sky, but for the first time that day, Ella felt a flicker of light breaking through the darkness.

They might only have a month, but they had hope, and sometimes, hope was enough to change everything.

Chapter 10
Treasures of the Past

Jada sat cross-legged on the carpet of Ella's living room, her tablet perched on her knees. The glow from the screen illuminated her face, the light flickering slightly as she scrolled through scanned images of the vault's books. Around her, the rest of the team watched in varying states of interest. Noah leaned against the wall, arms crossed, while Max sprawled out on the couch, tossing a tennis ball in the air. Ella sat beside Jada, her gaze fixed on the screen.

"This is taking forever," Max groaned, catching the ball one last time and sitting up. "You've been staring at that thing for hours. Are we any closer to uncovering the mysteries of the universe yet?"

Jada didn't look up. "If by 'mysteries of the universe,' you mean why this library is so important, then yes, we're getting there. Some of these dedications are... strange."

"Strange how?" Noah asked, stepping closer.

Jada tapped on the tablet, enlarging an image of a book's inside cover. The handwritten inscription read: *To Mae Carter, whose courage helped rebuild what was lost. Evelyn Blythe, 1942.*

Ella gasped softly. "Mae Carter. That's my grandmother. But what does she mean by 'rebuild what was lost'?"

"That's what I'm trying to figure out," Jada replied, swiping to another scanned image. "A lot of these dedications mention specific events—fires, floods, even wars. It's like these books weren't just donated; they were meant to commemorate something."

"Like a historical record," Noah said thoughtfully. "But instead of being written in a single book, it's spread across the whole collection."

"Exactly," Jada said, her excitement growing. "Look at this one." She pulled up another inscription. *To Marcus Thorne, who led the way home. Evelyn Blythe, 1945.* "This one was written after World War II. It's like each dedication tells part of a bigger story."

Max leaned over, peering at the tablet. "So you're saying these books are breadcrumbs? Like a history scavenger hunt?"

"Sort of," Jada said, though her tone was more serious. "But it's more than that. These dedications are tied to specific people and events in Blythewood's history. It's like Evelyn Blythe used the library to document the town's legacy."

Ella frowned, her mind racing. "If that's true, then these books are more than just keepsakes. They're proof of what this library has meant to the community over the years."

"And that's exactly why they need to stay here," Noah said, his voice firm. "If the developers get their hands on this collection, they'll split it up. Sell it. The history it represents will be lost."

Jada's fingers flew across the screen, pulling up another image. "Wait, this one's important." She enlarged the text, the words filling the screen. *To the people of Blythewood, who built this library from the ashes and gave it life. Evelyn Blythe, 1911.*

Ella leaned closer, her heart pounding. "The ashes? What ashes?"

"I think she's talking about the fire," Jada said, her tone growing serious. "There was a massive fire in Blythewood in 1910. It destroyed a lot of the town, including the old community center. The library was built as part of the town's recovery effort."

Noah nodded, his expression grim. "So the library isn't just a building. It's a symbol of resilience. It's a reminder of how the town came together after a tragedy."

"And Grayson wants to sell it off like it's nothing," Ella said bitterly, her fists clenching at her sides. "He doesn't care about what this place means to people."

Max tilted his head, a thoughtful expression crossing his face. "But what if we make people care? Like, really care. If we can connect these dedications to their families, their stories, they'll fight for the library. They won't let Grayson get away with this."

"That's a good point," Jada said, looking up at Max. "We could use the dedications to track down descendants of the people mentioned in the books. Imagine how powerful it would be to have them speak out about what the library means to their families."

Ella's determination grew as she nodded. "We need to act fast. Grayson's already set the clock ticking, and we're running out of time. Jada, keep digitizing the books and organizing the dedications. Noah, can you help me figure out the best way to present this to the town?"

"Of course," Noah said. "But we'll need more than just the books. We need a way to tie it all together, to show how the library connects everyone in the community."

"Leave the emotional stuff to me," Max said, cracking a grin. "I'll make sure people feel it in their hearts. And if that doesn't work, I'll guilt them into it."

Ella laughed despite the tension, the team's unity giving her a flicker of hope. "Alright, let's do this. The library's history isn't just words on a page. It's people. It's memories. And it's worth fighting for."

As they settled into their tasks, Ella couldn't help but feel the weight of the books' significance pressing down on her. They weren't just objects; they were pieces of the town's soul. And now it was up to her and her friends to protect them before it was too late.

The library's meeting room was a mess of papers, maps, and photographs strewn across the long wooden table. Jada's tablet glowed with images of the vault's contents, and a stack of Ella's handwritten notes sat precariously near the edge. Max leaned back in his chair, balancing it on two legs as he tossed a tennis ball in the air. Noah stood by the window, arms crossed, while Ella paced the room, her steps quick and deliberate.

"We have the pieces," Ella said, her voice firm. "Now we just need to figure out how to put them together."

"Easier said than done," Noah replied, turning to face her. "It's one thing to know the vault's contents are valuable, but convincing the town council? That's a whole other challenge."

"We can't just walk into their meeting and say, 'Hey, look at these cool books,'" Jada added, not looking up from her tablet. "They'll dismiss it as sentimental nonsense."

Ella stopped pacing and turned to the group, her hands on her hips. "So what do we do? We don't have time to wait around for the perfect solution. Grayson's already pushing his agenda, and every day we wait, the library gets closer to being sold."

"We go big," Max said suddenly, his chair landing back on all four legs with a thud. He tossed the tennis ball onto the table and leaned forward, his grin equal parts enthusiasm and mischief. "We put on a show. A community event, something that grabs everyone's attention."

Ella raised an eyebrow. "A show?"

"Think about it," Max said, gesturing animatedly. "We invite everyone—families, local businesses, anyone who's ever set foot in this library. We turn the vault into the centerpiece, showcase the books, the dedications, the stories behind them. Make it impossible for the council to ignore."

"It's not a terrible idea," Jada admitted, tapping her chin thoughtfully. "If we can get the community on our side, it'll put pressure on the council. They won't want to risk public backlash."

Noah frowned, his skepticism evident. "And how exactly are we going to pull that off? It's not like we can just slap together an event in a week."

"Why not?" Max shot back. "We've got the vault, we've got the books, and we've got Jada's tech wizardry. All we need is a little creativity and some elbow grease."

Ella nodded slowly, her mind racing. "Max has a point. If we can show people what the library means—what it's always meant—they'll fight for it. We just have to make it compelling."

"Compelling is easy," Max said with a wink. "I'm compelling just by showing up."

"Let's not rely on your charm alone," Noah said dryly. "We need a solid plan. First, we'll need to secure the vault. If people are going to see it, we have to make sure it's safe and protected."

Ella glanced at Jada. "Can you rig up a way to present the contents without letting anyone touch them? Like a digital walkthrough or a projection?"

Jada nodded, already jotting down notes on her tablet. "I can put something together. Maybe a slideshow of the dedications with voiceovers telling their stories. We'll need photos of the vault itself, too—something to give people a sense of the space."

"Great," Ella said. "What about logistics? We'll need to get the word out, set up the event, make sure we have enough space…"

"I'll handle that," Max volunteered. "Posters, flyers, maybe even a social media campaign. The whole town will know about this by the end of the week."

"You'll also need to think about security," Noah added. "If the developers or Grayson get wind of what we're doing, they could try to sabotage it. We can't let them interfere."

Ella's expression hardened. "Then we keep this quiet until everything's ready. No one outside this room knows what we're planning."

"Speaking of sabotage," Jada said, her brow furrowed as she scrolled through her tablet, "we need to make sure we don't lose control of the narrative. If Grayson spins this as sentimental overreach, we'll lose credibility."

"Which is why we keep it focused on the facts," Noah said. "The dedications, the historical significance, the connections to the town's past. We present it as irrefutable evidence that the library is worth saving."

"And we make it personal," Ella added. "The stories in those books aren't just history. They're people—families, memories, legacies. If we can make people see themselves in those stories, they'll fight for the library as hard as we are."

Max clapped his hands together. "Now we're talking. Let's make this the event of the century. We'll have the council in tears by the time we're done."

"I'll settle for a unanimous vote to save the library," Jada said, though a small smile tugged at her lips.

Ella looked around at her friends, a swell of gratitude and determination rising in her chest. "Alright," she said, her voice steady. "Let's do this. We've got a library to save."

The room buzzed with energy as the group dove into their respective tasks, the weight of their mission driving them forward. Ella couldn't shake the feeling that the stakes had never been higher, but for the first time, she also felt a glimmer of hope. Together, they had a plan. And together, they were going to make it work.

The library was eerily quiet that evening, its usual stillness now carrying a sense of unease. Ella sat at the large table in the center of the reading room, papers and photographs of the vault spread out before her. Jada was nearby, furiously typing on her laptop, while Max sat cross-legged on the floor, tossing a crumpled flyer into a wastebasket and muttering to himself. Noah leaned against the far wall, his arms crossed, his gaze distant.

"I'm telling you, this is bad," Noah said finally, breaking the silence. His voice was low but edged with tension. "If the wrong people find out about the vault, it won't matter how good our presentation is. They'll move faster than we can stop them."

Ella looked up, her stomach twisting. "What do you mean by 'the wrong people'? The developers?"

"Or Grayson," Noah said, his tone sharp. "Or anyone who thinks there's money to be made from what's in that vault. Do you know how quickly historical artifacts disappear when people realize they're valuable?"

"That's why we're keeping it quiet," Jada said, not looking up from her screen. "No one knows about the vault except us."

"And maybe the entire town by now," Max said, shooting his paper ball into the wastebasket with unnecessary force. "You heard those whispers at school today. Someone's been talking."

Ella froze, her fingers gripping the edge of the table. "What whispers?"

Max shrugged, but his expression was uncharacteristically serious. "Couple of kids were talking about a 'secret treasure' in the library. Said they overheard it from their parents. Didn't sound like they knew the details, but still…"

"Great," Noah muttered, running a hand through his hair. "So it's already out there."

Jada's typing stopped, and she looked up, her face pale. "If people are talking, it's only a matter of time before it gets to the developers. Or Grayson."

Ella stood abruptly, her chair scraping against the floor. "We can't let that happen. If Grayson finds out about the vault before we're ready, he'll twist it. He'll find a way to spin it so it works in his favor."

"But how do we stop the rumors?" Jada asked, her voice rising slightly. "We can't un-ring the bell."

"We don't stop them," Max said, surprising everyone. He leaned forward, his usual humor replaced by determination. "We get ahead of them. We take control of the story."

"And how do you suggest we do that?" Noah asked, his skepticism clear.

Max grinned, though there was no trace of mockery in it this time. "We make the vault the centerpiece of our event. We don't hide it; we highlight it. If the town knows the full story, if they see how much it means, no one will stand with Grayson."

"That's risky," Jada said, her fingers fidgeting with the edge of her laptop. "If we don't frame it perfectly, it could backfire."

Ella pressed her hands flat against the table, her mind racing. "But Max is right. The vault is our biggest weapon. If we don't use it, we lose any chance of showing the council and the town why the library matters."

"Then we need to act fast," Noah said, pushing off the wall. His voice was firm now, his earlier doubt replaced by focus. "The event has to happen sooner rather than later. The longer we wait, the more we risk losing control."

Jada sighed but nodded. "I can finish the digital presentation tonight. We'll need to print flyers, finalize the schedule, and make sure the vault is secure."

"I'll handle the flyers and the PR," Max said, standing and rolling up his sleeves. "I'll get the whole town to show up if it kills me."

Ella smiled faintly at his confidence, but her stomach churned with anxiety. "And I'll talk to Mrs. Pearlson. She can help us with the setup and make sure no one tries to access the vault before the event."

Noah glanced around the room, his gaze sharp. "We also need to keep watch. Someone has to be at the library at all times until the event. If word about the vault keeps spreading, it's only a matter of time before someone tries to get in."

"I'll take the first shift," Ella volunteered immediately. "I'm not leaving this place unguarded."

Jada raised a hand. "I'll stay with you. I can work on the presentation while we're here."

Max shrugged. "Fine by me. I'll take the next shift after I plaster half the town with flyers."

Noah nodded. "Good. Let's make sure we coordinate. No gaps, no slip-ups."

The group fell into a tense silence, the weight of their task settling heavily over them. Ella sat back down, her mind buzzing with worry and determination. The vault wasn't just a discovery anymore; it was a battleground, and they were fighting to protect it from forces that would destroy everything it represented.

"We can do this," Ella said finally, her voice steady despite the fear gnawing at her. "We've come too far to lose now."

Jada looked at her, a flicker of confidence returning to her expression. "Then let's make it count. If we're putting everything on the line, we're going to do it right."

Max grabbed his bag and slung it over his shoulder. "Time to rally the troops. I'll see you guys tomorrow."

As he left, Noah followed him to lock the doors, leaving Ella and Jada alone in the quiet library. The two girls exchanged a look, the gravity of their mission unspoken but deeply felt.

"We've got this," Jada said softly, as much to herself as to Ella.

Ella nodded, gripping the edge of the table. "We have to."

Chapter 11
Whispers in the Wind

The late afternoon light spilled through the library's tall windows, casting long golden beams that stretched across the reading room floor. Dust danced lazily in the shafts of sunlight, caught in the still air. The group had settled into their usual spots near the large oak table, their treasures spread out in careful disarray—journals, photographs, and the intricate model of Mrs. Blythe's dream library.

Noah sat at the edge of the table, his hands moving with a quiet focus as he turned the small wooden model over in his grip. His thumb traced the tiny carved roof, smoothing over the grooves left behind by someone else's careful hands decades before. There was a faraway look in his eyes, like he was somewhere else entirely.

Max leaned back in his chair, tossing a balled-up scrap of paper in the air and catching it again. "So… where do we even start? I mean, this stuff is amazing, but what's going to pull in the most money for the fundraiser?"

"The letters," Jada said without looking up, typing notes into her tablet. "And the blueprints. People connect with stories, and the blueprints tie it all together. They'll see what the library *could* be."

"And the model," Ella added, glancing at the miniature library still cradled in Noah's hands. "It's like holding Mrs. Blythe's dream in real life."

Noah didn't respond. His gaze lingered on the tiny windows of the model, his fingers hovering near the delicate woodwork.

"Noah?" Ella said softly, tilting her head. "You okay?"

He blinked, as if breaking out of a trance, and nodded slowly. "Yeah. Just… thinking."

Max looked at him, brows raised. "You've been staring at that thing for, like, fifteen minutes. You got something you want to share?"

Noah hesitated, setting the model gently down on the table. The quiet that followed felt heavy, expectant. Finally, he looked up, his voice low but steady. "This place… it reminds me of my grandfather."

Ella straightened. "Your grandfather?"

Noah gave a small nod, his eyes drifting back to the model. "Yeah. He used to bring me here when I was a kid. I didn't get it back then—I thought it was just books and a quiet room. But for him, it was more than that. He loved this library. It was where he came when he needed space to think."

Jada stopped typing, watching him carefully. "You've never mentioned that before."

Noah shrugged, a faint, nostalgic smile tugging at the corner of his mouth. "I guess I didn't think it mattered. But when we started finding all this—Mrs. Blythe's blueprints, the letters, the history—I remembered. My grandfather wasn't much of a talker, but he taught me everything I know about woodworking, right here in this library."

"In the library?" Max blinked, leaning forward. "What, did you two sneak tools in or something?"

Noah shook his head with a quiet chuckle. "No. He'd sit me down at the big table near the history shelves and show me how to sketch plans, how to measure angles, how to carve something beautiful out of a piece of wood. He'd bring his old tools, the ones he said had been passed down in our family, and he'd let me hold them. He always said, 'Anything worth building takes patience.'"

Ella's heart squeezed at the softness in his tone. "That's incredible, Noah."

"Yeah, well…" Noah looked down at the model again, his voice dropping. "After he passed, I didn't touch a carving knife for years. I didn't think I could. But being here now, seeing Mrs. Blythe's plans—it feels like… like I'm supposed to do something with it."

Max tilted his head, curiosity lighting up his face. "Do what, exactly?"

Noah glanced up at them, his expression steadier now, as if he'd made up his mind. "I'm going to build replicas of the things we've found—the treasures, the model, maybe even parts of Mrs. Blythe's unrealized plans. We can display them at the fundraiser, auction them off if we have to."

Jada blinked in surprise. "You mean, you'd carve them yourself?"

"Yeah." Noah nodded, his fingers brushing the edge of the model again. "My grandfather taught me how to do it right. If I can recreate the details—every curve, every angle—people will see what this library meant. It'll make them care."

Max let out a low whistle. "That's… ambitious. You're talking about building a mini-museum of stuff from scratch in less than a month."

"I can do it," Noah said firmly, meeting Max's gaze. "If it helps save the library, I'll do whatever it takes."

Ella leaned forward, her voice gentle. "Are you sure, Noah? That's a lot of work."

He looked at her, and something steady and unshakable flickered in his eyes. "I'm sure. This library gave my grandfather a place to share his craft with me. I owe it that much."

The room fell quiet again, but this time it wasn't heavy. It was full—full of purpose, of shared determination. Ella smiled softly, warmth spreading through her chest.

"That's incredible," she said. "We'll help however we can. You're not doing this alone."

"Yeah," Max chimed in, grinning. "I'll sand stuff or carry wood or whatever. You just tell me where you need me."

"I'll organize a display schedule," Jada added, already typing into her tablet. "If we get enough pieces together, we can feature them as part of Mrs. Blythe's exhibit."

Noah's lips quirked into a faint smile. "Thanks, guys."

Ella met his gaze, her voice steady. "Your grandfather would be proud, Noah. I know it."

Noah nodded, his fingers brushing over the miniature library again. "Let's make this count."

The sun dipped lower in the sky, its light fading to a warm amber glow across the reading room. The library felt alive around them, its walls holding onto their words, its stories pulsing through the air. Noah's resolve had ignited something in all of them—something unspoken but undeniable.

This wasn't just about saving the library anymore. It was about honoring the people who had made it what it was—people like Mrs. Blythe, and Noah's grandfather. They would build something worth remembering.

The Blythewood Library glowed faintly under the dim lights, its corners bathed in shadow as the night deepened outside. The creak of old chairs, the hum of Jada's tablet, and the occasional scrape of a pen against paper were the only sounds breaking the stillness. Scattered around the main reading room, the friends worked tirelessly, their determination pushing them through the exhaustion settling into their bones.

Ella sat hunched over a small stack of papers, her notebook open in front of her, the words she'd scribbled barely legible now after countless rewrites. Her pen hovered midair as she read aloud softly to herself, testing the rhythm of the sentences. "The library isn't just part of our history… It's a cornerstone of our future."

"Too formal," Max called from across the room, his voice muffled as he rifled through a cardboard box full of supplies. He stood up suddenly, holding a spool of twine in one hand and an old cloth banner in the other. "No offense, El, but you sound like you're trying to run for president."

Ella sighed, looking up at him with an exhausted smile. "I'm trying to sound convincing, Max. This speech has to get through to people who don't think the library matters."

"Yeah, but you also need them to feel something," he replied, crossing the room to sit on the floor near her. "Talk to them like you talk to us. Tell them what it means to you. Not just why it's important."

Jada's voice drifted over from the other side of the table, where she sat surrounded by her tablet and a half-dozen printed photos. "Max actually has a point for once."

"Hey!" Max shot back, mock-offended, but Jada ignored him.

"Ella, remember how you talked about the library the first time we found the letters?" Jada continued, adjusting the digital layout of an exhibit with sharp, focused movements. "You said it was like a home for stories. People will connect to *that*—not statistics or timelines."

Ella leaned back, letting their words settle in as her fingers traced the edges of her notebook. "So… speak from the heart," she said softly.

"Exactly," Noah said from his spot near the far corner. He was hunched over a workbench he'd set up, surrounded by pieces of wood and tools. The quiet sound of his sanding had filled the background for hours. "The mayor and the council need more than facts. They need to understand what this place feels like to you—to all of us."

Ella nodded slowly, flipping the page to start over once more. "I can do that."

Max dropped the twine and banner next to a pile of paint cans and brushes. "And while you work on being all inspirational and whatnot, I'm going to make sure these banners look perfect." He gave a cheeky grin, rolling up his sleeves. "Never underestimate the power of good signage."

"Just don't spell anything wrong this time," Jada muttered without looking up, smirking faintly.

Max pointed dramatically at her. "That was one time, and 'commnunity' *still* looked pretty great in cursive."

Jada didn't bother responding, too focused on finalizing the exhibit designs she was arranging on her tablet. She flicked through mockups of the blueprints, the letters, and the photographs, carefully placing each item into a layout that balanced history with impact. "I've got Mrs. Blythe's blueprints in the center, surrounded by the journals and artifacts. The letters will be framed on the walls so people can read them up close."

Noah glanced over, pausing mid-sand. "You're creating a timeline?"

"Kind of," Jada replied, tapping the screen. "I want people to see the past and present together. That way, when they look at Mrs. Blythe's vision, they can picture it coming to life. It has to feel real."

"It *is* real," Ella said softly, more to herself than anyone else. She looked at her notebook, the words she'd written no longer feeling like a jumble. "We just have to show them."

The hours slipped by unnoticed as they worked. Max spread banners across the floor, carefully painting bold, confident lettering. Jada finalized her exhibit plans, printing out mockups and notes for how everything would look. Noah's steady hands shaped wood into small replicas, the rhythm of his tools as comforting as a heartbeat. And Ella wrote, the quiet scratching of her pen carrying the weight of everything she wanted to say.

At some point, Max broke the silence, sitting back to examine his work. "You know what's crazy? We're actually doing this."

Jada didn't look up, still adjusting her photos. "What's crazy is that we don't have a choice. If we don't do this, no one else will."

Noah wiped the sawdust from his hands, glancing over at Ella. "How's the speech coming?"

Ella looked up, smiling faintly. "Better. It's not perfect, but… it's honest."

Max grinned, tossing a paintbrush onto the tarp. "Then it's perfect. People are going to listen to you, El."

"Let's hope so," she said quietly, but there was strength in her voice.

Outside, the night deepened, the stars beginning to stretch across the dark sky. Inside the library, the air was warm, the faint scent of lavender lingering as though the building itself was listening. For the first time in weeks, they felt closer than ever to the finish line.

Jada stood up and stretched, rolling her shoulders. "Alright, I think I'm done for tonight. If I keep staring at this screen, I'll start seeing letters in my sleep."

Max flopped onto his back, letting out a dramatic groan. "Same. My hands smell like paint and regret."

Noah stood, stacking his tools neatly. "We made good progress. Tomorrow, we keep going."

Ella set her pen down, her speech finished, at least for now. She looked at her friends—exhausted but smiling—and felt a flicker of hope, like a light in the dark.

"We'll make it work," she said softly. "We don't have much time, but it's enough."

Max sat up, flashing her a grin. "Captain Carter, always the optimist."

Jada chuckled, and Noah gave a small nod of agreement.

Together, they packed up their things, the quiet hum of the library following them as they moved. The walls seemed to watch, as if the library itself knew how hard they were fighting. And as they left for the night, Ella looked back one last time, whispering to herself, "We're almost there."

The library was a patchwork of organized chaos. Banners half-painted lay across the reading room floor, carefully outlined sketches of Mrs. Blythe's vision sprawled across tables. Bits of sawdust from Noah's latest wooden carvings clung to the edge of a workbench, and Jada's tablet sat charging on a chair nearby, its screen frozen on an exhibit layout. The room felt alive, like the library itself had absorbed their energy and held it close, warm and unyielding.

In the middle of it all, Ella sat cross-legged on the floor, an open notebook perched on her knees, though her pen had long since been set aside. The others were scattered around her, backs against chairs or crates, every bit as drained as they were satisfied with their progress. The room was quiet save for the soft hum of the overhead lights and the faint creaks of the library settling for the night.

Max stretched his arms overhead, flopping dramatically against a pile of folded drop cloths. "I think we've earned, like, three weeks of sleep after tonight."

Jada snorted without looking up, swiping through photos on her phone. "Three weeks? Try three hours. We've still got so much to do."

"Jada," Max said, lifting his head with mock seriousness, "let me dream. I'm a delicate creative soul, and I require proper rest."

Ella smiled, shaking her head as she closed her notebook. "Delicate isn't exactly the word I'd use, Max."

"Rude," Max shot back, though his grin betrayed him. "But I'll let it slide because I'm too tired to argue."

Across the circle, Noah leaned back against one of the wooden crates, a small carving of a tiny book held between his hands. He rubbed a thumb along its edges, the faint beginnings of a smile softening his usually serious expression. "You're the least delicate person I know."

"See? Noah gets me," Jada said, smirking as she nudged Max with her foot.

"Traitor," Max muttered, throwing his hands up before grinning wide.

The laughter that followed was soft and genuine, echoing faintly against the tall shelves. For a brief moment, the tension and exhaustion fell away, leaving only the warmth of their shared company.

Ella glanced around at them, a flicker of gratitude filling her chest. They were tired, yes—stretched thin by long nights and looming deadlines—but they were here, together. The weight of what they were trying to do felt lighter somehow when shared.

"You know," Jada said, breaking the quiet, "it's kind of crazy how far we've come."

Max propped himself up on one elbow, tilting his head. "You mean how we went from nosy treasure hunters to full-on 'Save the Library' crusaders?"

"Exactly," Jada replied, her smirk softening into something warmer. "I mean, a month ago, we weren't even sure what we were looking for. And now… look at this place." She gestured around the room, taking in the banners, the exhibits in progress, the wooden models lined neatly along Noah's workspace. "It's starting to feel like we're really making a difference."

"We are," Noah said quietly, his gaze steady. "Even if the town doesn't see it yet, they will."

Ella nodded, her voice soft but certain. "Because we're not just showing them what the library was—we're showing them what it can still be."

Max grinned, leaning back again. "And because we're awesome."

Jada rolled her eyes, but she didn't argue. Instead, she tucked her phone away and settled back into her seat, her shoulders visibly relaxing for the first time in hours. "Well, I'll give you this: we make a good team."

"The best team," Ella said with a smile, looking at each of them in turn. "We couldn't have come this far without all of us."

Max pointed dramatically at the ceiling. "Team Library forever!"

Noah smirked. "You're not carving that into the library wall, Max."

"I wasn't planning on it," Max replied, though his grin suggested otherwise.

The group fell into another round of quiet laughter, the sound carrying through the stillness like the crackle of a warm fire. Ella leaned her head back against the base of a chair, staring up at the ceiling as the library's soft glow wrapped around them.

"We're really going to do this, aren't we?" she murmured, almost to herself.

"Yeah," Noah said, his voice steady and calm. "We are."

"And we're going to make it *great*," Jada added, her determination sharp even in her exhaustion.

Max stretched his legs out across the floor, crossing his arms behind his head. "Great? Please. We're going to make history."

Ella closed her eyes for a moment, letting the quiet settle again. The bond between them was unspoken but strong, forged by late nights, shared frustrations, and moments like this—when the weight of their fight felt lighter simply because they carried it together.

"We'll make her proud," Ella whispered, almost too softly to hear.

Noah glanced at her, his brow lifting slightly. "Who?"

"Mrs. Blythe," Ella replied, opening her eyes. She looked at the others, her voice filled with quiet certainty. "I think she'd be proud of us."

The library seemed to hum around them then, as if agreeing—its walls holding their laughter, their stories, and their promise. The night stretched on, but for now, they didn't feel tired.

They felt unbreakable.

Chapter 12
The Gathering Storm

The streets of Blythewood were quiet, bathed in the soft glow of the old streetlamps that flickered now and then, as if unsure of their place in the night. Mayor Grayson walked with his hands in the pockets of his overcoat, his polished shoes echoing faintly against the cracked sidewalk. The air was cool and still, carrying the faint scent of rain that lingered from earlier in the evening.

He hadn't meant to take this route, but his feet seemed to have a will of their own. And now, here he was—standing in front of the Blythewood Library.

The building loomed ahead of him, its familiar silhouette outlined against the dark sky. The windows were dark except for one—just one—where a faint light flickered softly, as though the library itself refused to fully sleep.

Grayson stopped on the sidewalk, his gaze lifting to the tall, arched windows.

"You're still awake too, huh?" he muttered, half to himself, half to the building.

The wind stirred, rustling the old leaves on the ground, but no other answer came. Still, something about the quiet hum of the place settled around him like a presence, heavy yet strangely comforting.

He let out a slow breath, shaking his head. "Ridiculous," he murmured. "It's just a building."

But the words rang hollow, even to him.

A faint memory tugged at the back of his mind, unbidden—himself as a young boy, no more than eight or nine, standing right where he stood now. The library doors had seemed impossibly tall back then, like they guarded a secret only he could uncover.

"Keep up, Henry!" his mother's voice had echoed from behind him, light and teasing. "You can't spend all day staring at the door."

He remembered the way he had gripped her hand and walked inside for the first time, how the scent of old books and polished wood had hit him like a wave. It was the smell of stories, of possibility.

Grayson exhaled sharply, shoving the memory aside as he glanced up at the lone glowing window. *They're just kids,* he thought. *What do they know about reality?*

And yet, their voices from the meeting played in his head—Ella Carter's most of all.

"The library isn't just bricks and shelves. It's history, it's community, and it's people."

Her words had been clear and determined, so much like another voice from his childhood—Mrs. Blythe's, standing behind the library desk with her kind but sharp eyes. *"The library's doors are always open, Henry. For anyone who needs them."*

He shook his head again, as if he could banish the ghosts of his past by sheer will.

"I'm trying to do the right thing," he muttered, his voice barely above a whisper. "For the town. For everyone."

Another gust of wind pushed against him, carrying the faintest trace of lavender. Grayson froze, his brow furrowing as he turned slightly, scanning the empty street.

"Lavender…" he murmured, almost to himself.

It had been her scent—Mrs. Blythe's. She'd always worn it. He could still remember walking into the library as a boy, trailing his fingers over the spines of books while that soft, floral fragrance lingered in the air, calming him.

"You're letting nostalgia get the better of you," he said aloud, though his voice wavered.

His gaze returned to the dark windows, his mind spiraling back to the afternoons he'd spent at the long oak tables, head buried in books he was too young to understand. Mrs. Blythe would always stop by, a book tucked under her arm, and say, "Pick a story you *want* to read, Henry. The rest will come later."

Grayson turned on his heel, muttering under his breath, "It's a library. Nothing more."

He took a step away—then another. But he couldn't seem to leave. His shoulders slumped as he turned back to face the building again, glaring at it like it had offended him.

"I don't have a choice," he said, though the conviction in his voice had thinned. "The developers' offer… it's what's best for everyone."

The library, as always, remained silent.

But somehow, in the hush of the night, it felt as if the building *heard* him—and disagreed.

For a moment, Grayson allowed himself to stand there in the stillness. He let the memories linger this time—the afternoons spent lost in books, the quiet joy of discovery, and Mrs. Blythe's unwavering belief that stories mattered.

His resolve cracked, just a little.

"Maybe," he whispered, "they're not wrong."

The words hung in the air for a moment before he turned once more, this time walking away from the library with slower, heavier steps. But as he disappeared into the night, the faint glow from the lone window remained, steady and unyielding.

And somewhere deep inside, a seed of doubt had been planted.

The library's reading room had been transformed into their makeshift stage, its soft glow fighting against the encroaching dusk outside. Banners lined the far wall, some half-finished with Max's bold lettering still drying, while Jada's display boards rested upright against the tables, waiting for the real event. In the center, Ella stood behind a small lectern they'd borrowed from storage, her notebook open in front of her.

"Whenever you're ready, Captain," Max said, sprawling dramatically on a nearby chair.

"Don't call me that," Ella muttered under her breath, though a flicker of a smile betrayed her nerves. She tightened her grip on the notebook and glanced at her friends—Max, leaning back with a grin that screamed support; Jada, seated with her tablet balanced on her lap, watching carefully; and Noah, standing near the shelves, his arms crossed but his nod subtle and reassuring.

"Take a breath," Jada encouraged softly. "It's just us."

Ella nodded, inhaling deeply. "Okay. Here goes."

She straightened her shoulders, the paper in her hand crinkling slightly as she began.

"This library isn't just a building," she said, her voice soft at first, like testing the waters. "It's more than walls and bookshelves. It's a legacy."

She paused, her eyes flicking up to the empty room as if imagining the faces that would fill it soon.

"Mrs. Blythe built this place because she believed in stories— not just the ones in books, but the ones we carry with us. The people who found hope here, the kids who learned to dream here… those stories matter."

Her voice quivered slightly on the word "dream," and she clenched the notebook tighter, willing herself to steady.

"This library gave people a home," she continued, her tone gaining strength. "A place where no one was turned away. Whether you needed to lose yourself in a book or just sit somewhere quiet, the doors were open. Always."

She glanced up at Max, Jada, and Noah. They weren't just watching her—they were with her. That thought pushed her forward.

"And I know what some people say: that it's just a building, just a collection of old books. But they're wrong. This library has *soul.* Every letter we found, every blueprint, every word Mrs. Blythe left behind proves it. She believed that the library could grow, could become something even greater—just like the people who walk through its doors."

Ella's voice caught slightly, and she looked down at the notebook again. For a split second, the silence threatened to swallow her whole.

"You've got this, El," Max said softly, his voice just loud enough for her to hear.

She nodded once and looked up again, locking eyes with an empty spot on the far wall, as if the mayor and council were already there.

"This library is part of who we are. It's memories and dreams and second chances all wrapped together. And if we lose it—if we tear it down for something that will never matter the same way—then we lose a part of ourselves."

Jada's tablet clattered softly as she set it down, watching Ella with something close to pride.

"Saving this library isn't about saving the past," Ella finished, her voice clear and unwavering now. "It's about building a future that remembers where we came from. It's about believing that some things are worth fighting for, no matter how impossible they might seem."

She exhaled, her last words hanging in the air like the faint echo of a bell.

For a moment, no one spoke. Then Max let out a low whistle, sitting up in his chair. "Okay, Captain Carter. That was incredible. Goosebumps level incredible."

Ella blinked, her cheeks warm as she let out a shaky laugh. "You're just saying that."

"No, he's not," Noah said, stepping closer. "That was powerful, Ella. If you deliver it like that at the fundraiser, they won't be able to ignore you."

Jada nodded in agreement, her expression serious. "Your voice shook a little, but that's not a bad thing. It made it real. People are going to hear you and *feel* it."

Ella swallowed, finally letting her shoulders relax as she sat back on the edge of the lectern. "I don't know. I just… I hope it's enough."

"It *will* be," Max said confidently. "Because you're not just reading words—you believe them. And people can tell the difference."

Jada smirked faintly. "For once, I agree with Max."

"Shocking," Max quipped, but his grin was genuine.

Noah placed a hand on Ella's shoulder, his voice calm. "You're doing exactly what Mrs. Blythe would've wanted. You're giving the library a voice."

Ella looked at each of them, the weight of the moment settling in her chest. They were tired, and the fight ahead was far from over, but this moment—this rehearsal—felt like a step forward.

"Thanks, guys," she said quietly, her voice steady now. "I couldn't do this without you."

Max threw his arms wide. "We're Team Library, El. You're stuck with us."

The group laughed softly, the tension breaking as the library's silence wrapped around them once more. Ella glanced back at the lectern, her speech still clutched in her hand, and for the first time, she believed it.

They were ready.

The library was bathed in the golden glow of late afternoon sunlight, the warmth spilling through the tall windows like a gentle embrace. Ella, Max, Jada, and Noah sat in their usual spot near the large oak table, surrounded by their preparations for the fundraiser—painted banners, exhibit layouts, and Noah's wooden carvings carefully placed in boxes.

Max sat with his feet up on a chair, twirling a paintbrush in his fingers. "So, what's the over-under on the mayor actually showing up for Library Day?"

"Zero," Jada said flatly, tapping at her tablet as she adjusted a display plan. "Grayson doesn't care. He's already made up his mind."

"Don't say that," Ella replied, though her voice lacked the confidence she hoped for. "We don't know that."

"We *do* know that," Jada shot back, glancing up. "He hasn't listened to a word we've said, no matter how much proof we've shown him. It's like talking to a brick wall."

Max shrugged, leaning back further. "Maybe we need to borrow a wrecking ball. Metaphorically, of course."

Before Ella could respond, the familiar sound of slow footsteps reached their ears, and Mrs. Pearlson appeared in the doorway. The librarian moved with a deliberate calm, carrying a small tray of steaming mugs, the faint scent of chamomile and honey wafting through the air.

"You've all been at it for hours," Mrs. Pearlson said gently, setting the tray down on the table. "Take a moment to breathe, won't you?"

"Thanks, Mrs. Pearlson," Noah said softly, taking a mug and blowing gently on the tea.

"Chamomile," Max mused, sniffing his mug. "Perfect for stressed-out teenagers saving a library."

Mrs. Pearlson chuckled as she eased herself into a chair at the table, her eyes twinkling with quiet affection as she took in the group. "You're doing something incredible here. Don't let doubt creep in."

Ella smiled faintly, wrapping her hands around the warm mug. "We're trying. It's just... it feels like the mayor's already decided. How are we supposed to change his mind if he won't even listen?"

Mrs. Pearlson tilted her head, her expression thoughtful. "You might not need to change his mind entirely," she said softly. "Sometimes, all it takes is a moment of doubt—a small crack in the armor—for someone to start seeing things differently."

"What do you mean?" Jada asked, looking up from her tablet.

The librarian's gaze turned toward Ella. "I saw him last night, you know. Mayor Grayson."

That caught everyone's attention. Max nearly spilled his tea as he sat forward. "Wait, what? He was *here*?"

"Not inside," Mrs. Pearlson corrected, folding her hands neatly in her lap. "But he was standing just outside, lingering by the steps."

"Why?" Noah asked, his brow furrowing.

Mrs. Pearlson smiled faintly, her voice taking on that knowing tone only someone who'd seen years pass could carry. "I imagine he was remembering."

"Remembering what?" Ella pressed, sitting up straighter.

"What this place once meant to him," Mrs. Pearlson said simply. "Henry Grayson wasn't always a mayor weighed down by numbers and budgets. When he was a boy, he spent many afternoons here, lost among the shelves, just like you all."

"Seriously?" Max blinked, his voice incredulous. "Grayson? Library kid?"

Mrs. Pearlson chuckled. "Oh yes. Mrs. Blythe often teased him about being a permanent fixture. He'd sit right at the big table by the history section with piles of books—sometimes ones far too advanced for him. But he loved it here. This library was his sanctuary."

The room fell quiet for a beat as her words settled over them.

Ella's voice was soft when she spoke. "Then why doesn't he care now?"

"Time does strange things to people," Mrs. Pearlson replied, her tone gentle. "Responsibilities change priorities. But that doesn't mean the memories are gone. Seeing the library again— seeing the fight you're putting up—might be stirring something in him. A part of him that still remembers."

Jada leaned forward, resting her elbows on the table. "You think there's still hope?"

"I do," Mrs. Pearlson said firmly. "A man who takes time to stand and look at a place he claims to have written off isn't so sure of his own decision. Perhaps all he needs is a reason to believe again."

Max grinned, pointing at Ella. "Well, good thing we've got Captain Carter and her speech of the century ready to hit him right in the feels."

"Max, stop calling me that," Ella muttered, though she couldn't help but smile.

Noah nodded, his expression thoughtful. "If Mrs. Pearlson's right, we've got a chance. Even if it's small, it's enough."

Ella looked down at her hands wrapped around the mug, her chest filling with something warm and hopeful. "If he remembers what this library used to mean to him, maybe he'll see what it can still be."

Mrs. Pearlson smiled, a glimmer of pride in her gaze. "Exactly. You're doing more than saving a building, Ella. You're reminding people of something they've forgotten. That's more powerful than you know."

The room fell quiet again, the faint hum of the library surrounding them like a steady heartbeat. Outside, the sunlight began to fade, but inside, hope lingered like the warmth of Mrs. Pearlson's tea, spreading through them all.

For the first time in days, it felt like the tide was shifting—just a little. And sometimes, a little was all you needed.

Chapter 13
Voices of Blythewood

The library was alive in a way it hadn't been in years. The normally quiet halls now buzzed with the sound of voices, laughter, and footsteps echoing across the polished wood floors. Families crowded together near the entrance, while children tugged on their parents' hands, eager to see the mysterious "hidden treasure" they had heard so much about. A small stage had been set up near the biography section, with a projector casting an image of the vault onto a white screen. Jada stood at the control table, her fingers flying across her laptop as she adjusted the presentation.

Ella stood at the center of the room, scanning the crowd with a mixture of pride and nervous energy. The turnout was even larger than they'd hoped. People of all ages had come, from longtime patrons who remembered the library's golden years to younger residents who had barely set foot inside before tonight. Max stood beside her, flashing grins and shaking hands like a seasoned politician.

"Look at this," Max said, nudging Ella with his elbow. "I told you the town would show up. All they needed was a little nudge from yours truly."

Ella smiled despite her nerves. "You did good, Max. We all did."

Noah approached from the side, his expression guarded but hopeful. "Everything's ready. Mrs. Pearlson is about to start her speech."

Ella nodded, her stomach twisting in knots. "Do you think it'll be enough?"

Noah placed a steadying hand on her shoulder. "It'll be enough. People are here because they care. Now it's up to us to show them why they need to fight for this place."

The hum of the crowd quieted as Mrs. Pearlson stepped onto the small stage. Her presence commanded attention, and even the restless children seemed to settle. She adjusted her glasses and looked out over the crowd, her voice trembling slightly as she began to speak.

"Good evening, everyone," she said, her words carrying through the room. "Thank you all for being here tonight. It means more than I can say to see so many familiar faces—and so many new ones—as we gather to celebrate what this library has meant to our town."

She paused, her gaze sweeping across the crowd. "This library isn't just a building. It's a living, breathing piece of Blythewood's history. It's where generations have come to learn, to dream, to connect. And tonight, we want to share with you something extraordinary—something that has been hidden for far too long."

The screen behind her flickered, and an image of the vault appeared. The crowd gasped, murmurs rippling through the room as the camera panned over the shelves of rare books and their intricate dedications.

"These books," Mrs. Pearlson continued, "are more than just words on paper. They are pieces of our past, left by those who came before us. Each dedication tells a story—a story about resilience, about community, about the heart of Blythewood itself."

Jada clicked through the slideshow, pausing on specific dedications as Mrs. Pearlson read them aloud. The room was silent except for her voice, and more than one person could be seen wiping away tears.

"To Mae Carter," Mrs. Pearlson read, her voice soft but steady. "Whose courage helped rebuild what was lost. To Marcus Thorne, who led the way home. To the people of Blythewood, who built this library from the ashes and gave it life."

Ella glanced at the crowd, her chest tightening as she saw the impact the words were having. People weren't just listening— they were feeling it. They were remembering.

When Mrs. Pearlson stepped down, a man from the crowd raised his hand. Ella recognized him as Mr. Peterson, the owner of the town's hardware store. "My grandfather used to talk about that fire," he said, his voice thick with emotion. "He always said the library was the first thing they rebuilt because it gave people hope. It was the one place that brought everyone together."

A woman stepped forward, holding the hand of a young boy. "My mother used to bring me here every week," she said. "She always said the library was where she found her strength after my dad passed. I didn't understand it then, but I do now."

The floodgates opened. One by one, members of the community stepped forward to share their stories, their memories of the library and what it had meant to them. Each story added weight to the argument Ella and her friends had been trying to make for weeks: that the library wasn't just a building. It was a lifeline.

From the corner of the room, Ella spotted Mayor Grayson, his arms crossed as he watched the event unfold. His usual polished demeanor was cracked, his expression unreadable as he listened to the stories. When one elderly woman tearfully recounted how Mrs. Blythe herself had taught her to read as a child, Grayson shifted uncomfortably, his gaze dropping to the floor.

Ella leaned toward Noah, whispering, "Do you think we're getting to him?"

Noah's lips twitched into the faintest of smiles. "It's hard to ignore the truth when it's staring you in the face."

The event continued, each story adding another layer to the library's importance. By the end of the night, the room felt charged with determination. As the crowd dispersed, Ella stood by the door, shaking hands and thanking people for coming. Many left with promises to attend the council meeting and speak out against the sale.

When Grayson finally approached, Ella straightened, her heart pounding. He looked at her for a long moment, his expression unreadable, before finally speaking.

"You've made your point, Ella," he said, his voice quieter than she'd expected. "I'll see you at the meeting."

As he walked away, Ella exhaled, a mix of relief and resolve washing over her. They weren't done yet—not by a long shot. But tonight, they had given the town something to believe in. And that was a victory in itself.

The council chamber was packed to capacity, a murmur of voices rising and falling like the rustle of wind through leaves. Ella stood near the front, clutching the edges of her notes so tightly her knuckles were white. Beside her, Mrs. Pearlson adjusted her glasses, her presence a calming anchor in the storm of Ella's nerves. Behind them, the community members who had spoken so passionately at the event the night before filled the rows of chairs, their faces set with determination.

Mayor Grayson sat at the center of the council's long table, flanked by four council members. His expression was unreadable, his hands clasped in front of him as he surveyed the room. To his left, Councilwoman Dillard leaned forward, whispering something to the councilman beside her. Ella caught the faintest flicker of doubt in Dillard's posture and held onto it like a lifeline.

Grayson raised a hand, calling for order. The room quieted, the weight of the moment settling over everyone.

"This meeting is now in session," Grayson began, his voice steady but lacking its usual confidence. "We are here to decide the fate of the Blythewood Public Library. As you all know, the council has reviewed the financial implications of maintaining the library versus the benefits of selling the land to developers. Tonight, we will vote to determine its future."

A murmur rippled through the crowd, but it quickly subsided as Grayson's gaze swept the room.

"Before we proceed," Grayson continued, his tone clipped, "we will hear from Ella Carter, who has requested to speak on behalf of the library."

Ella swallowed hard, her pulse racing as she stepped to the podium. Her legs felt shaky, but as she turned to face the room, the sight of so many familiar faces—Mrs. Pearlson, Max, Jada, Noah, and the townspeople who had rallied behind them— gave her courage.

She took a deep breath and began. "Thank you, Mayor Grayson, council members, and everyone here tonight. I'm Ella

Carter, and I'm here to talk about what the Blythewood Library means—not just to me, but to this town."

Her voice trembled slightly, but she pressed on. "The library is more than just a building. It's a piece of our history, a place where our stories live. When we uncovered the vault, we found books that hold dedications from generations of Blythewood residents. Each one tells a story about resilience, about hope, about the heart of this community."

Ella's eyes scanned the room, meeting the gazes of the audience. "To some of you, those stories might not seem important. But they are. They're reminders of who we are and where we've come from. When the town faced hardships—a fire, a flood, a war—the library was there. It was a place where people came together to rebuild, to heal, to dream of a better future."

She turned back to the council, her voice gaining strength. "If we sell the library, we're not just losing a building. We're losing a piece of ourselves. We're telling the next generation that history doesn't matter, that the stories of those who came before us can be erased. And once it's gone, we can't get it back."

Councilman Harris, who had been vocal about selling the library, shifted in his seat, his expression unreadable. Ella took a deep breath, steadying herself for her final plea.

"I know the financial challenges are real," she said, her tone softening. "But there are other ways to solve them. Ways that don't involve selling off the soul of Blythewood. The library is worth fighting for. It's worth saving. And I hope you'll see that too."

Ella stepped back from the podium, her heart pounding. The room was silent for a moment, then a ripple of quiet applause broke out. She turned to see Mrs. Pearlson smiling at her, pride shining in her eyes.

Grayson cleared his throat, bringing the room back to order. "Thank you, Miss Carter. The council will now deliberate."

Councilwoman Dillard leaned into her microphone. "Mayor Grayson, I'd like to speak before the vote."

Grayson's expression tightened, but he nodded. "The floor is yours."

Dillard turned to address the room. "I'll admit, I came into this meeting ready to vote for the sale. I thought it was the practical choice, the only choice. But last night, at the event Miss Carter and her friends organized, I was reminded of something important. Practicality is important, yes, but so is heart. So is history. And this library has both."

A murmur of agreement ran through the crowd as Dillard continued. "I've changed my mind. I will be voting to save the library."

Ella's chest tightened with hope as she turned back to the council. One vote in their favor—but it wasn't over yet. Her eyes flicked to Grayson, whose expression remained stony.

The roll call vote began. Councilman Harris hesitated before casting his vote to sell, but Ella's heart leapt when Dillard's firm "save" countered it. The third vote was another "sell," and the fourth—a younger councilman who had attended the event—voted to save.

All eyes turned to Grayson. His was the deciding vote.

The room was thick with tension as Grayson sat back in his chair, his fingers steepled under his chin. For a long moment, he said nothing, his gaze sweeping over the crowd, lingering on Ella. She held her breath, her hands clenched at her sides.

Finally, Grayson exhaled and leaned into his microphone. "I vote to save the library."

The room erupted in applause and cheers. Ella felt tears prick her eyes as relief and joy washed over her. She turned to Mrs. Pearlson, who pulled her into a tight embrace.

"You did it," Mrs. Pearlson whispered. "We did it."

As the crowd celebrated, Ella caught a glimpse of Grayson slipping out of the room, his expression conflicted. She didn't know what had swayed him in the end, but it didn't matter. The library was safe—for now. And they had proven that, together, a community's voice could make all the difference.

The cheers had begun to die down, but the energy in the room lingered like the last chords of a triumphant song. Ella stood among her friends, her heart swelling with pride and relief. Around them, the townspeople buzzed with conversation, a renewed sense of hope weaving through their voices. The library was safe—for now.

Mayor Grayson's voice cut through the din as he addressed the room again. "Order, please. I understand this is an emotional moment, but I must remind everyone that while the library has been preserved, there are conditions."

The celebratory murmurs faded as the crowd turned their attention back to the council. Ella's stomach tightened. Of course, there was more to it.

"The council's decision includes certain stipulations," Grayson continued, his tone firm but measured. "The library's operations must become financially sustainable within the next year. This includes increasing community involvement, securing additional funding, and ensuring the building is properly maintained. Without progress on these fronts, this decision will be revisited."

A ripple of unease spread through the crowd. Ella glanced at Mrs. Pearlson, whose expression remained calm but resolute.

"What does that mean?" Max muttered beside her, his usual bravado dampened. "We have to keep proving ourselves?"

"It means the fight isn't over," Jada said quietly, her voice edged with determination. "We've bought time, but we still have work to do."

Grayson's gaze swept the room, lingering briefly on Ella and her friends. "This library is an important part of Blythewood's history," he said, his voice softer now. "But its future depends on all of us. The council has done its part. Now it's up to this community to show that the library truly matters."

The room was silent for a moment, the weight of his words settling over everyone. Then Mrs. Pearlson stepped forward, her voice clear and unwavering. "We will do it. This community has already shown that it cares about this library, and I know we can rise to the challenge."

Applause broke out again, quieter this time but no less heartfelt. Ella exchanged a glance with Jada, Max, and Noah, their shared determination sparking between them.

As the meeting adjourned and the crowd began to disperse, Ella's friends gathered around her. "So," Max said, breaking the silence with a grin, "looks like we're not off the hook yet."

"Did you think this was going to be easy?" Noah asked, his tone teasing but warm.

"I didn't think we'd get a homework assignment after saving the library," Max retorted, earning a laugh from Jada.

Ella smiled, though her thoughts were already racing. "It's not just about the library anymore," she said. "It's about the community. If we can get everyone involved—make them feel like they're part of this—we'll succeed."

"Sounds like a lot of work," Max said, though his grin softened the words.

"It is," Jada agreed, "but it's worth it."

Mrs. Pearlson approached, her hands clasped in front of her. "You've all done something remarkable," she said, her voice thick with emotion. "But Ella is right. The real work is just beginning. I have no doubt that this town can rise to the occasion—but it will need leaders. And that's where you come in."

Ella blinked, surprised. "Us?"

"Yes, you," Mrs. Pearlson said firmly. "You've shown what's possible when people care enough to fight for something. That's a rare quality, and this community will look to you for guidance. Don't underestimate what you've started."

Ella felt a wave of both pride and responsibility wash over her. "We won't let you down," she said quietly.

"I know you won't," Mrs. Pearlson replied, her smile warm and reassuring.

As the group began to leave, they found themselves drawn back to the biography section, where their journey had truly begun. The vault remained hidden behind its secret door, but its presence felt almost tangible, like a heartbeat beneath the surface.

"I feel like we should check on it," Ella said softly, her gaze fixed on the shelf that concealed the entrance.

The others nodded, and together they moved to the spot. Noah expertly found the hidden latch and opened the panel, revealing the narrow doorway. One by one, they stepped inside, their flashlights cutting through the dimness.

The vault was just as they'd left it, the shelves lined with books, each one a testament to the library's legacy. Ella took a deep breath, the cool air carrying a faint, familiar scent—lavender.

"Do you smell that?" Jada asked, her voice hushed.

"Yeah," Max said, his usual humor absent. "It's like… flowers. Lavender, right?"

Ella felt a shiver run down her spine, but it wasn't fear. It was something deeper, something comforting. She placed her hand on one of the shelves, her voice barely above a whisper. "Mrs. Blythe."

The others exchanged glances but said nothing, the weight of the moment settling over them. Ella closed her eyes, the scent growing stronger as if in silent acknowledgment of everything they had done.

When they finally left the vault, Ella turned to her friends, her expression resolute. "We've done something amazing," she said. "But we're not done yet."

"Not even close," Noah agreed, his usual seriousness softened by a small smile.

"Good," Max said, slinging an arm around Ella's shoulders. "Because I was starting to think life was getting boring."

Jada chuckled. "Let's make sure it stays interesting, then."

As they stepped back into the library's main hall, Ella felt a quiet sense of purpose settle over her. The library was safe, for now, but its future was in their hands. And together, she knew they could handle whatever came next.

Chapter 14
The Deciding Vote

The Blythewood Library had never felt so alive. From the moment the sun broke over the sleepy town, the air had been electric, a current of anticipation weaving through the streets. By mid-morning, people were arriving in waves—families, shop owners, students, and retirees, all drawn to the old stone building that stood like a sentinel in the heart of Blythewood.

Outside, hand-painted banners waved gently in the breeze. **"Blythewood Library Day: A Celebration of Stories"** stretched across the front steps, while smaller signs—carefully crafted by Max—lined the walkway, inviting people inside.

Ella stood just inside the doors, her heart pounding as the steady hum of conversation and laughter reached her ears. The library buzzed with energy in a way it hadn't in years. She watched as a group of kids darted into the children's section, already oohing over a reading corner Jada had set up. Near the entrance, Mrs. Pearlson welcomed visitors with a warm smile, her cardigan dusted with specks of confetti from the opening banner Max had insisted on.

"It's working," Ella whispered to herself, barely believing what she was seeing.

"It's *more* than working," Max said beside her, bouncing on his heels. He gestured dramatically to the room. "Look at this! The place is packed. I mean, we're basically celebrities now."

Jada smirked as she walked up, holding her tablet tightly to her chest. "Don't get too comfortable, Max. We still have a lot to do. The live readings start in fifteen minutes, and Mrs. Hayworth's poetry group is already looking for their spot."

"Let them at it," Max replied, grinning. "I'm just here to soak up the vibes. This is next-level library magic."

"Focus," Ella said, though she couldn't help but smile. "Where's Noah?"

"Setting up the artifacts in the back room," Jada replied, glancing toward the far hall. "He wanted everything to look perfect."

Ella nodded, her gaze drifting over the crowds. The exhibits were already pulling people in. Framed letters, carefully organized photographs, and the replica models Noah had built were displayed on tables and along the walls. A group of older residents lingered by Mrs. Blythe's journals, pointing and murmuring with admiration as they traced the old, looping handwriting.

"Look at them," Ella said softly. "They're actually *seeing* it. Mrs. Blythe's dream."

Jada's expression softened, and she placed a hand on Ella's shoulder. "That's because of you, Ella. You got us here."

"*We* got us here," Ella corrected, smiling gratefully. "This wouldn't have happened without all of us."

Before Jada could respond, a voice rose over the hum of the crowd. "Everyone, gather around! Our first performance is starting in the main reading room!"

Ella turned to see Max waving his arms like an overenthusiastic carnival barker. "You've got to see this, people! It's history and drama all rolled into one!"

"Max, stop yelling," Jada called after him, though her tone lacked any real bite.

"Hey, it's working!" Max shouted back, grinning as a wave of people followed him toward the reading area.

Ella shook her head, laughing softly. "He's ridiculous, but he's not wrong."

They moved to the main reading room, where chairs had been arranged in neat rows facing a small podium. A student from the local high school stood nervously at the front, clutching a copy of one of Mrs. Blythe's letters. As the room settled into an expectant hush, she began to read.

"*'To those who find comfort in these walls...'*"

The words echoed through the space, wrapping around the crowd like a familiar embrace. Faces softened, shoulders relaxed, and for a moment, it was as though Mrs. Blythe herself stood among them, whispering her dreams back into the world.

Ella caught sight of Noah in the doorway, quietly observing the scene with a faint, proud smile. He met her gaze, nodding once as if to say, *We're doing it.*

As the reading continued, Jada leaned closer to Ella, speaking just above a whisper. "Do you see who's standing in the back?"

Ella turned slightly, her breath catching. Mayor Grayson stood near the rear of the room, hands clasped behind his back. His expression was unreadable, but he stayed rooted in place, watching the performance with a quiet intensity.

"Do you think—?" Ella began, but Jada cut her off gently.

"Don't overthink it. Just let him see."

Ella exhaled slowly, forcing herself to focus. The mayor's presence wasn't a victory—not yet—but it was something.

The applause that followed the reading brought Ella back to the moment. Max bounded forward again, hands clapping loudly. "Give it up for our first reader! And don't forget—there's more where that came from! Live performances all day, folks!"

The crowd laughed softly, and Ella watched as they began to scatter—some to the artifact displays, others to the children's corner or the refreshment table where Mrs. McNally had set out a spread of cookies and lemonade.

"This is really happening," Ella murmured, mostly to herself.

"It is," Noah said, stepping up beside her. "And it's just the beginning."

Ella looked out over the library—alive, full of voices, stories, and laughter—and for the first time, she felt something beyond hope.

She felt certainty.

The hum of voices filled the Blythewood Library as people crowded into the main reading room, now transformed into the centerpiece of the fundraiser. Rows of chairs stretched out in front of a small wooden podium, the air buzzing with curiosity and expectation. The artifacts were carefully arranged behind the podium—Mrs. Blythe's journals, Noah's carved replicas, and the framed deed of protection, each one a silent testament to the library's legacy.

Ella stood just off to the side, her palms pressed against her notebook. She could feel the thrum of her heartbeat in her fingertips, but she forced herself to breathe.

"You've got this, El," Max said quietly, squeezing her shoulder. He flashed a grin, his voice light. "Channel your inner hero. You know, the one who yelled at me for spilling soda on your notes last month."

Ella rolled her eyes, but the corner of her mouth twitched into a smile. "Thanks, Max."

"Time to make history," Jada added, stepping closer. Her usual sharp tone softened. "They're here for you now. You just have to remind them why they care."

Ella looked to Noah, who nodded once, his steady presence grounding her. "Speak from the heart," he said simply.

The crowd began to settle as Mrs. Pearlson stepped up to the podium, raising her hands for quiet. "Thank you, everyone, for coming today," she said warmly. "It brings me such joy to see this library alive with voices once more. Today, we celebrate not just stories, but the people who make them possible." She turned, smiling at Ella. "And now, I'd like to introduce someone who has worked tirelessly to bring us here—Ella Carter."

A wave of applause swelled, and Ella's feet moved before her mind caught up. She stepped toward the podium, her fingers gripping the edges as the room seemed to stretch out in front of her. The faces blurred together—neighbors, friends, strangers—but one stood out.

Mayor Grayson. He lingered near the back, hands clasped in front of him, his expression unreadable but softer than Ella remembered.

Her heart stilled for a beat before she drew in a deep breath and began.

"This library has always been more than just a building," Ella said, her voice clear and steady despite the tremor she felt inside. "It's a home. A sanctuary. A place where people come to dream, to learn, and to belong."

She paused, letting the words settle. The crowd quieted, their attention focused on her.

"Many of you know Mrs. Blythe, the woman who built this library. But what you might not know is that she didn't just leave us a building—she left us a vision. In her journals, her letters, and her plans, she dreamed of a library that would grow with the town, a place that would always be here for anyone who needed it."

Ella glanced at the table of artifacts behind her, her confidence growing.

"She believed so much in that dream that she found a way to protect it. The deed we discovered proves it—this library belongs to *you,* the people of Blythewood. It can't be taken away unless we allow it."

Murmurs rippled through the crowd, but Ella pressed on, her voice rising.

"This library isn't just part of our history. It's part of our future. It's where children find stories that inspire them. It's where students discover worlds beyond their own. It's where people like my friends and me learned that stories aren't just in books—they're in us. They're in this community."

She paused, scanning the crowd. Her gaze landed on Mayor Grayson, and to her surprise, he was watching her with an intensity that sent a spark of hope through her. His face, so often impassive, seemed softer now, as though her words had reached him in a way she hadn't thought possible.

"This isn't about choosing between the past and the future," Ella continued, her voice gentler now. "It's about *building* a future that remembers who we are. Mrs. Blythe gave us this library because she believed in Blythewood. She believed in *us.*"

The room was silent now, save for the faint creak of chairs as people leaned in to listen.

"We have a choice," Ella finished, her voice steady. "We can let something irreplaceable slip away, or we can stand together to save it. The library belongs to all of us—and it's time we fight for it."

A beat of silence followed her words, the kind that held the weight of something unspoken. Then, someone began to clap—one pair of hands, then another, until the room erupted into applause.

Ella exhaled sharply, her hands shaking slightly as she stepped back from the podium. She caught Jada's approving nod, Max's wide grin, and Noah's quiet smile.

But it was Mayor Grayson who held her gaze. He hadn't moved, his expression unreadable but softer still, like a wall that had begun to crack. And in that moment, Ella knew she'd done what she could.

As the applause filled the library, the weight on her chest lifted. They weren't just fighting for the library anymore—they were fighting for each other, for their town, for something bigger than themselves.

And now, Blythewood was listening.

The hum of excitement hadn't dimmed since Ella's speech. The Blythewood Library felt like the heart of the town again, alive with voices and energy. Children laughed in the reading corner while others wandered the exhibits, their fingers trailing over Noah's carved replicas and the glass-covered displays of Mrs. Blythe's journals. Near the refreshments table, Mrs. McNally refilled trays of cookies, beaming as she chatted with neighbors about "those incredible kids and their hard work."

Ella stood near the donation box by the front doors, watching as people—*her* people—dropped bills, checks, and even jars of loose change inside. Each soft *clink* of coins, each rustle of paper filled her with a growing sense of wonder. It was happening.

"Look at this," Max said, striding up with an exaggerated grin as he pointed to the overflowing donation jar. "I haven't seen this much money in one place since the last school bake sale."

Jada walked up beside him, tablet in hand, her voice tinged with disbelief. "We're actually doing it. People are giving so much—some even more than we asked for." She held up the tablet screen, where the numbers were climbing faster than she could keep up.

"Are we close?" Ella asked, hope cracking through her words.

"Close?" Jada shook her head, a smile finally breaking across her face. "Ella, we've *already* passed what we needed to start restoration. And people are still donating."

Ella's breath caught, the weight of their efforts lifting like fog in the morning sun. "We did it…"

"We totally did it," Max whooped, pumping his fist into the air. "Team Library for the win!"

Noah appeared from the back room, his hands still lightly dusted with sawdust from setting up the last of his displays. He didn't need to ask—he could tell by their expressions. "We made it?"

Ella turned to him, unable to hold back her smile. "We did. The fundraiser worked."

Before Noah could respond, a voice rang out through the crowd. "Everyone, can I have your attention?"

The hum of conversation stilled as all eyes turned toward the front. Mayor Grayson stood near the entrance, his presence commanding but his expression softer than usual. For the first time in weeks, there was no air of dismissal about him.

Ella's heart skipped.

"I want to thank all of you for being here today," Grayson began, his voice steady. "This library has been a part of Blythewood for generations, and what I've seen here today reminds me why." He paused, scanning the room before continuing. "This isn't just a building. It's a cornerstone of this community. A place of learning, of growth, and of history. You've all proven that it still matters."

A murmur of agreement swept through the crowd, but the mayor's eyes sought out Ella's, holding her gaze.

"I won't deny that I had doubts," he said, his voice quieter now, though it still carried. "But seeing the outpouring of support here today—seeing what this library means to you all—has reminded me of something I nearly forgot. When I was a boy, I sat at these tables, just like many of you have. I lost myself in books, in stories, and in the possibilities they gave me. And those memories are worth protecting."

He turned fully to face the crowd. "You've done something extraordinary today. You've come together, you've raised funds, and you've proven that Blythewood isn't willing to let go of its roots."

The room seemed to hold its breath.

"So, as mayor," Grayson declared, "I pledge my full support to the restoration of the library. The council will back this project, and we'll ensure the developers' bid is turned away. This library isn't going anywhere."

For a beat, there was silence—an almost stunned stillness. Then, the room erupted in cheers. Applause thundered through the space, filling every corner with the sound of triumph.

Max let out a whoop, throwing an arm around Ella's shoulder. "Captain Carter, you did it!"

Ella let out a shaky laugh, her chest tight with relief and joy. "*We* did it."

Jada turned to Noah, shaking her head in disbelief. "Did you hear that? The mayor's backing us."

Noah smiled faintly, his gaze on Ella. "I knew he'd come around."

As the cheers continued, Mayor Grayson stepped forward to Ella, his expression unreadable at first. "Miss Carter," he said, his tone softer than she'd ever heard it. "You were right. This library *does* have a soul. And it's thanks to you—and your friends—that we'll get to see it live on."

Ella met his gaze, her voice steady. "It's thanks to everyone here. Mrs. Blythe believed in this library, and now the whole town does too."

Grayson gave her a small nod of approval before stepping back to address the crowd once more.

Ella turned to her friends, her voice light despite the tears threatening at the corners of her eyes. "This library is safe. We did it."

Max fist-pumped again, his grin wide. "I think Mrs. Blythe would be pretty proud of us right about now."

Jada smiled, her tablet momentarily forgotten. "She would. And so should we."

Noah looked around at the crowd—at the neighbors and families who had come together, united by a cause—and nodded. "This is what community looks like."

Ella took it all in—the smiles, the laughter, the renewed life of the library—and felt it deep in her bones. Mrs. Blythe had built this place to bring people together, and now, decades later, it was doing exactly that.

As the sun dipped lower outside the tall windows, its light spilling across the room like a golden promise, Ella knew this was only the beginning. The library would live on, its doors open for the generations to come.

And for now, that was enough.

Chapter 15
A Future to Fight For

The Blythewood Library stood bathed in the soft morning light, its worn stone façade catching the first golden rays of the sun. For the first time in decades, scaffolding hugged its sides like a protective frame, workers in hard hats moving purposefully across the grounds. The faint clang of hammers and the buzz of saws filled the air—not as noise, but as a symphony of progress.

Ella stood at the edge of the lawn, hands tucked into the pockets of her jacket, her eyes taking in the transformation. The faded, neglected building now felt alive again, as though it could breathe for the first time in years. The front doors—once weathered and creaking—had been removed for restoration, while the windows were being cleaned and replaced, their panes glinting faintly in the rising light.

Max jogged up beside her, a grin already plastered across his face. "This place looks like it's getting a glow-up of epic proportions."

Ella smirked, her voice soft with awe. "It really does."

From behind them, Noah's voice chimed in as he approached, a stack of design sketches tucked under his arm. "Wait until you see the new plans up close. The reading garden is already halfway mapped out. It's going to be incredible."

"The *reading garden*," Ella repeated, the words like music to her ears. She turned to Noah, a smile breaking across her face. "Mrs. Blythe would've loved that."

"She planned it first," Noah replied with a small nod, holding up one of the sketches. The paper rustled slightly in the breeze. "We're just finishing what she started."

"Finishing and upgrading," Jada added as she walked over, tablet in hand, already pulling up blueprints and photos. "The art wing alone is going to bring in visitors. Workshops, exhibits, even spaces for the community to display their work. This isn't just a library anymore—it's a hub for the whole town."

Max whistled low, his hands settling on his hips. "Imagine that. From 'almost bulldozed' to 'best place in Blythewood.' I love a good comeback story."

Ella laughed softly, glancing back at the building. The rusted clock tower that had loomed dark and silent for so long was now scaffolded, too, its restoration nearly complete. The workers had promised that by the end of the week, its long-stilled gears would turn again, and its chimes would echo across the town just as they had when Mrs. Blythe first dreamed of this place.

"It doesn't even feel like the same building," Ella said quietly, a note of wonder in her voice.

"It isn't," Jada replied with a knowing smile. "It's better."

A new sound suddenly broke through the morning air—a deep, steady creaking that made all four of them pause.

"Wait…" Max said, holding up a hand. "Is that…?"

The creaking grew louder, followed by a distant whirring that rumbled up through the tower.

"No way," Noah murmured, his eyes snapping up to the clock face above.

All four of them turned in unison, watching as the clock's hands—still tarnished but unmistakably moving—began to shift for the first time in decades. The rumbling grew steadier until, finally, the sound they'd been waiting for echoed across Blythewood.

The chime.

A low, melodic note rang out, deep and rich, carrying over rooftops and through the sleepy streets of town. The group froze, the sound washing over them like a wave, as people began to step out of shops and houses to listen.

"It's working," Ella whispered, her throat tightening.

The clock chimed again, the sound layered with a kind of magic that only something restored to life could hold. Max let out a triumphant laugh, punching the air. "Would you *listen* to that? Blythewood, the library is *back*."

Jada glanced at Ella, her expression softer now. "You did this, you know. You made this happen."

Ella shook her head, though she was smiling. "We all did."

From across the lawn, Mrs. Pearlson appeared, walking slowly up to the group with a look of pride etched onto her face. She stopped beside Ella, tilting her head back to listen to the chimes as they rang out again.

"It's been a long time since I heard that sound," Mrs. Pearlson said softly. "It's as though the library is waking up again."

"It is," Noah replied, his voice steady but filled with warmth. "And it's here to stay."

Ella turned to face the library one more time, taking in the scaffolding, the workers, the gardens being prepared along the sides of the building—everything. What had once felt fragile now stood strong, rooted not just in bricks and mortar, but in history and the love of the people who believed in it.

The clock rang out a final time, its echo lingering as the morning air stilled. For a moment, no one said anything. Then, Ella spoke, her voice soft but certain.

"This is only the beginning."

Max grinned. "And it's gonna be epic."

Jada smirked, already tapping at her tablet. "We'll need to host a grand reopening. Something to let the whole town see what they've built."

Noah nodded, a quiet smile tugging at his lips. "We'll make sure it lasts for generations."

The four of them stood together, side by side, watching as the workers continued their work, each step forward a promise kept. The Blythewood Library was no longer a forgotten relic—it was a place reborn, filled with light, laughter, and stories waiting to be written.

And somewhere in the soft breeze that swept across the lawn, carrying the last echoes of the clock tower's chime, it almost felt as though Mrs. Blythe herself was watching, smiling proudly as her dream finally came to life.

The afternoon sun warmed the newly restored lawn of the Blythewood Library, casting a golden glow over the gathering crowd. Families, students, and lifelong residents stood shoulder to shoulder, their voices hushed in anticipation. The library, once a crumbling relic, now stood proud—windows gleaming, wood polished, and scaffolding gone. The clock tower had chimed earlier that morning, a sound that had brought the town to a halt, heads lifting in wonder as if hearing a promise fulfilled.

At the top of the library steps, Ella stood beside Mrs. Pearlson, Max, Jada, and Noah, her hands clasped tightly in front of her.

A velvet curtain hung over the center of the façade, hiding what lay behind it. In front of the steps, a crowd had formed, faces familiar and unknown, all of them waiting. Ella could see the mayor standing toward the back, his posture formal but his face far softer than the first time he'd stood here.

Mrs. Pearlson took a step forward, her cardigan rippling slightly in the breeze as she raised her hands to quiet the murmuring crowd.

"Welcome, everyone," she said warmly, her voice carrying across the lawn. "Today, we stand together to honor not just a building, but a legacy—a place that has held our stories, our dreams, and our memories."

The crowd fell into a stillness that felt reverent. Ella looked out and caught the gaze of familiar faces: Mrs. McNally from the diner, the teachers who'd volunteered at the fundraiser, kids from school sitting cross-legged at the front.

Mrs. Pearlson turned slightly to face Ella, her eyes glimmering with pride. "None of this would have been possible without the determination of a small group of people who reminded us why this library matters."

Ella felt her cheeks flush as the crowd turned to look at her, Max nudging her gently from the side. "Say something," he whispered with a grin.

Ella took a step forward, her voice soft but steady. "We fought for this library because we knew it was worth saving. It isn't just a place for books—it's a home for dreams, for memories, and for every person who steps through its doors. This library belongs to all of us—our past, our present, and now, our future."

She paused, her throat tightening as she tried to keep the emotion from spilling over. "Mrs. Blythe believed in this place. She believed in *us*. And today, we get to honor her dream and build something even greater."

A gentle murmur of agreement rippled through the crowd, quiet but powerful. Ella glanced over at Jada, who gave her a small nod of approval, and then at Noah, whose steady gaze was filled with pride.

Mrs. Pearlson stepped forward once more, resting her hand on the curtain's edge. "And so, we dedicate this plaque, a promise to all who enter—now and for generations to come."

With a small tug, the velvet curtain fell away, revealing a gleaming bronze plaque set against the stone. The words etched into it reflected the sunlight, bold and clear:

"Blythewood Library—For the people who built it, and those who keep it alive."

The crowd broke into soft applause, but the sound barely registered for Ella. She stared at the plaque, her vision blurring slightly as tears welled in her eyes. Max was the first to notice, nudging her shoulder.

"You're crying," he teased softly, though his voice held no mockery. "I knew you were a softie."

Ella laughed through the tears, wiping at her eyes. "I'm not crying. I'm just… overwhelmed."

"It's okay," Jada said quietly, stepping closer. "We all are."

Noah nodded, his voice calm. "It's everything we hoped for."

Ella looked at them—her friends who had been there through every impossible moment, every late night, every failure and triumph. The library had brought them together, but it had given them more than that: a purpose, a shared dream, and a bond that would last long after the doors reopened.

The applause grew louder, sweeping through the crowd like a wave. People stepped closer to read the plaque, to touch it gently as though the words carried some quiet magic. Ella spotted Mrs. McNally, dabbing her eyes with a handkerchief, and saw kids pulling at their parents' sleeves, asking questions about what the library had been and what it would become.

Toward the back, Mayor Grayson stood quietly, his expression unreadable at first—but when he caught Ella's eye, he gave her a small, respectful nod.

"This is just the beginning," Mrs. Pearlson said softly, her voice just for Ella and the others. "The library has woken up again. And it's because of you."

Ella let out a shaky breath, the weight of it all settling over her like warmth. She looked back at the plaque, the words a promise they had kept.

"For the people who built it, and those who keep it alive."

As the sun climbed higher in the sky, casting light across the crowd, Ella smiled, tears still glistening in her eyes. The library was alive again—its story ready to be written, page by page, for generations to come.

The late afternoon sunlight filtered through the library's restored windows, casting long golden streaks across the polished wood floors. The plaque gleamed proudly at the entrance, surrounded by flowers people had left behind—small tokens of gratitude from townspeople who'd come to see what they had saved.

Ella, Max, Jada, and Noah stood quietly in the main reading room. The crowd had gone, the library now settling into a calm hush as though it, too, was taking a deep breath after everything. Around them, the shelves looked cleaner, the walls brighter, and the air carried the faint scent of lavender mixed with sawdust—new beginnings layered with the library's history.

Max broke the silence first, flopping onto one of the sturdy wooden tables, letting out a dramatic sigh. "Okay, can we just agree we're heroes now? Like, small-town legends? Because I'm pretty sure I deserve a statue."

"You want a statue in the library?" Jada shot back, raising an eyebrow as she sat on the edge of a chair. "It'll have to be life-sized. Hard pass."

"Fine," Max replied, grinning. "I'll settle for a plaque next to Mrs. Blythe's."

Noah smirked, shaking his head. "You'd be lucky to get a sticky note."

"Hey!" Max pointed a finger at him, though his smile never wavered. "I'm just saying, one day when they write a book about all this—"

"We'll make sure you get a special chapter," Ella interrupted, her voice warm with laughter. She leaned against the back of a chair, her gaze soft as it swept across the room.

The group fell quiet again, but this time it wasn't awkward or heavy. It was comfortable, the kind of silence that only came when words weren't necessary. For weeks, they'd poured their hearts into saving this place, and now they stood in its restored beauty, a reflection of their work and their bond.

Noah's voice broke the quiet, thoughtful and steady. "It's strange, isn't it? To think about how close we came to losing all of this."

Ella nodded, her fingers brushing the edge of the nearest table. "I keep thinking about Mrs. Blythe. All those plans, all those dreams she had for the library… and how close they were to being erased."

Jada looked up from her tablet, where she'd been quietly sketching out a new design for the art wing's layout. "But they weren't. Because of us. Because we believed it was worth saving."

"And because we didn't give up," Noah added, his voice steady. "Even when it felt impossible."

Max sat up, his usual grin softening into something more serious. "You know, for all my complaining and near-death experiences—"

"You had one near-death experience," Jada corrected with a smirk.

"Fine. For all my *one* near-death experience," Max continued, rolling his eyes. "This was worth it. Every second. We didn't just save a library. We made history."

Ella smiled at him, then looked around at each of them. "We did more than that. We gave the library a future. Mrs. Blythe started it, but now it's ours to carry on."

Jada leaned back, crossing her arms. "So, what happens now? We go back to school, back to normal life, and pretend we didn't just fight to save a piece of history?"

Noah shook his head, his gaze firm. "It's not over. Just because we saved the library doesn't mean the work stops. There's always more to do."

Ella stepped closer to the center of the room, her voice quiet but filled with certainty. "Then we make a promise. Right here, right now. To protect the library's legacy, to make sure it stays alive for future generations."

Max stood, brushing imaginary dust from his shirt. "You want us to make, like, an official vow?"

Ella smiled. "Why not? We didn't come this far just to walk away now."

Jada glanced at Noah, then back to Ella. "Fine. But if we're doing this, let's make it real."

The four of them moved to stand together in a loose circle, right at the heart of the reading room. The late light streamed down on them, filtering through the tall windows like a blessing.

Ella looked at each of them, her voice steady. "We promise to protect the library's story, to honor its past and build its future."

"We promise," Noah echoed quietly.

"To keep fighting for what matters," Jada added.

Max placed a hand over his heart dramatically. "And to make sure no one forgets how awesome we are in the process."

Jada groaned, rolling her eyes, but her smile betrayed her amusement.

Ella laughed softly, then added, "And we promise to always believe in places like this—a home for stories, for dreams, and for people."

The words hung in the air for a moment before Noah nodded, his expression serious. "We'll make sure it lasts."

"We'll make Mrs. Blythe proud," Jada added, her voice quieter now.

Max grinned, looking around at his friends. "Team Library forever, huh?"

"Forever," Ella replied, her voice full of warmth.

They stood there for a moment, the library around them humming with life, the weight of their promise settling into something both unspoken and unbreakable. They had saved this place, but they had saved something in themselves, too— a belief in possibility, in each other, and in the stories that deserved to live on.

As the sun dipped lower, the chimes of the clock tower rang out again, clear and steady, echoing across the town. And standing together in the quiet glow of the Blythewood Library, they knew their journey had only just begun.

Epilogue
The Living Library

The Blythewood Public Library stood bathed in the warm glow of a setting sun, its once-faded grandeur now restored by the hands of a community that had fought to save it. The newly polished oak doors gleamed with pride, and the stained-glass windows sparkled as if each pane celebrated the life teeming within.

Inside, the library hummed with activity. Children gathered in the newly refurbished reading corner, their laughter and curiosity mingling with the rhythmic tapping of keyboards and the rustle of turning pages. Above it all, the faint, comforting scent of lavender drifted through the air, like a whisper of approval from the past.

Ella Carter stood near the biography section, her hand resting on the edge of the shelf where her journey had begun. The secret panel was no longer a secret, though it had been carefully preserved as part of the library's new interactive exhibit. A plaque nearby told the story of the vault, the hidden books, and the group of friends who had uncovered them.

Max strolled up beside her, balancing a stack of books in one hand and a cup of coffee in the other. "You're not still staring at that plaque, are you?" he teased. "It's starting to look suspicious."

Ella rolled her eyes but smiled. "I was just thinking about how it all started. It feels like a lifetime ago."

"Don't get too nostalgic," Max said, nudging her with his elbow. "You'll make me cry, and I've got a reputation to uphold."

"Sure you do," she replied, laughing softly. "How's the tech station coming along?"

"Jada's got it under control," Max said, nodding toward the far corner of the library. Jada stood at a sleek, modern workstation surrounded by eager students learning how to digitize the library's collection. "She's practically a wizard at this stuff. I just stand nearby and pretend I know what I'm doing."

Ella followed his gaze, her chest swelling with pride. "She's incredible. This whole place is."

"It's because of you, you know," Max said, his tone uncharacteristically serious. "You're the one who made all this happen."

Ella shook her head. "It wasn't just me. It was all of us—Jada, Noah, Mrs. Pearlson, the whole town. This place wouldn't be here without everyone's help."

"Don't be so modest," Max said, his grin returning. "You're the heart of Team Library. You always have been."

Before Ella could respond, the sound of applause rippled through the room. She turned to see Noah standing at the front of a small crowd, holding up an old, leather-bound book. He was leading a workshop on book preservation, his quiet passion drawing smiles and nods from his audience.

"Look at him," Max said, shaking his head. "Who knew Mr. Serious had such a way with people?"

"He's always had it," Ella said softly. "He just needed a reason to show it."

As the applause died down, Mrs. Pearlson approached, her silver hair pinned neatly back and her eyes twinkling with pride. "Ella," she said, her voice warm and familiar. "It's good to see you enjoying yourself."

"I wouldn't be anywhere else," Ella replied, hugging the librarian. "How's the rare books room holding up?"

"Better than I expected," Mrs. Pearlson said, smiling. "The community's been incredibly respectful. It's clear they understand how important those books are now. Thanks to you."

Ella flushed, but before she could reply, a group of children burst into the room, laughing and chattering as they made their way to the reading corner. One of them—a girl no older than seven—paused near Ella, her wide eyes filled with wonder.

"Are you the one who saved the library?" the girl asked shyly.

Ella crouched down to her level, smiling. "I was part of a team. A lot of people helped."

The girl's face lit up. "Thank you. This is my favorite place."

Ella's throat tightened, but she managed to nod. "Mine too."

As the girl ran off to join her friends, Ella stood and looked around the library. It was alive again, more vibrant than she had ever dared to hope. The books in the vault were now part of a rotating exhibit, drawing visitors from neighboring towns and sparking new interest in Blythewood's history. Events and workshops filled the calendar, and the library had become the bustling hub of the community once more.

Ella took a deep breath, letting the sounds of the library wash over her. For a moment, she thought she caught the faintest scent of lavender and heard a whisper on the air—a voice she imagined might belong to Evelyn Blythe, saying, *Well done.*

The library was safe, its stories preserved and its soul intact. And though Ella knew there would always be challenges ahead, she felt ready to face them, surrounded by the friends and the community that had made this place so much more than just a building.

It was home.

www.ingramcontent.com/pod-product-compliance
Lightning Source LLC
Chambersburg PA
CBHW060534160726
47991CB00001B/324